THE 7th PASSENGER

AN ALASKA THRILLER

ALASKA THRILLERS SERIES

BOOK THREE

Andrew Cunningham

Copyright © 2024 by Andrew Cunningham
All Rights Reserved
No portion of this book may be reproduced in any form without written
permission from the publisher or author, except as permitted by U.S. copyright law.
ISBN-9798324735388

Books by Andrew Cunningham

Thrillers
Deadly Shore

Alaska Thrillers Series
Wisdom Spring
Nowhere Alone
The 7th Passenger

Yestertime Time Travel Series
Yestertime
The Yestertime Effect
The Yestertime Warning
The Yestertime Shift

"Lies" Mystery Series
All Lies
Fatal Lies
Vegas Lies
Secrets & Lies
Blood Lies
Buried Lies
Sea of Lies

Eden Rising Series
Eden Rising
Eden Lost
Eden's Legacy
Eden's Survival

Children's Mysteries
(as A.R. Cunningham)
The Arthur MacArthur Mysteries: The Complete Series

To Charlotte … my love

Prologue

ANCHORAGE, ALASKA—OCTOBER 1966

The snow had just begun to fall.

Chat looked up, mesmerized by the large flakes in the night sky. Night sky! There seemed to be a lot of night sky up here. Locals told him that this was nothing. It was only October. Check back in late December if Chat wanted to see what dark really looked like.

No thanks. He didn't. Chat had seen enough of Alaska in the three days they'd been there—three days of bone-chilling cold. Sure, the concert had been a success, but that was to be expected. *The Wonder Boys* had sold out every concert for the last eight months. They were one of the most popular bands in America, with their distinctive blend of rock and roll, and country.

But Chat could see the writing on the wall—something he hadn't told the band simply because they would never understand it.

Chatwell "Chat" Olson was the band's manager. At 39, he was twenty years older than the band members. He had discovered Arlo, Frankie, and Holt at a county fair in Iowa. Normally, he wouldn't have made a trip to Iowa under any circumstances, but a friend had tipped him off about a small band called *The Country Boys*. Stupid name. That would be the first thing to change, assuming they were as good as his friend said.

They were. These young men could sing. Arlo was the lead singer and guitarist, and Frankie played the drums. Holt played bass and was also the band's songwriter, and there was none better. He rivaled the top names in the business.

What the band didn't have was a way out of Iowa. Chat provided that way. First, he had to get them to trust him, which they did without question as soon as he told them how far they could go in the business. Then, he had to change the band's name. It had to be something with a little more pizzazz. *The Wonder Boys* seemed to do the trick.

The problem was that while musically, they could live up to the name, in every other way, they were severely lacking. They had the personalities of rocks. They were small-town hicks who had talent—massive talent—but zero charisma. Chat had a challenge on his hands.

Chat had them concentrate on the recording studio for the first few months of their collaboration. He quickly got them a contract with one of the biggest labels. But the record label owner saw what Chat had seen—that these boys needed polishing… a lot of polishing! They had to have something more than talent to draw in their audience.

In those months, the band recorded two albums. Three of their singles reached the Top Ten, and the masses clamored for the band to hit the road.

Well, Chat had done his best. He taught them a few tricks to enhance their stage presence and entertain the crowds. It seemed to be enough. Their fans loved them. But it didn't change the fact that Arlo, Frankie, and Holt were dumb as stumps. Chat knew that their meteoritic rise to the top would eventually end up with them crashing and burning, especially since they had recently discovered drugs. In the short span of eight months, fame and money had corrupted them despite Chat's efforts to keep them focused.

However, there was another factor that was destined to put an end to their careers. This was the part they would never understand. It was called The British Invasion. Bands like the Beatles and the Rolling Stones were bringing new life to rock and roll. Not only were the bands good, but they had band members who possessed personalities. Their fans didn't just know them as bands; they could relate to the musicians individually. They cared about what Paul, John, and George were into. They loved the quirkiness of Ringo. Mick's energy on stage captivated his audiences. These bands were charismatic, charming, and funny. *The Wonder Boys* were ... well ... not.

Now, they were headed to Fairbanks. It was a favor to one of the promoters. He had promised some colleagues in Fairbanks that he'd get *The Wonder Boys* to give a benefit concert. At least, that's what they were supposed to be going there for. But Chat knew that there was another reason. He didn't know the reason, but he had accepted a large sum of money from the promoter to do the concert—and to keep his mouth shut. Hey, it wasn't his concern. This guy was providing the plane and the pilots free of charge. It couldn't get any better than that.

And so what if the trip was just a handy diversion for

something else? The boys were clueless, so they would be fine. All they had to do was give their concert.

Chat would fly to Seattle and meet them there in a couple of days. He figured Arlo, Frankie, and Holt could do this concert without him. After all, how hard could it be? They would do their thing and head to Seattle later the next day.

Chat watched as the band members and three roadies climbed into the DeHavilland Canada DHC-6 Twin Otter.

"Behave yourselves," Chat yelled to them.

They waved to him with big smiles on their faces. They were going on a trip without their mother hen.

A minute later, another man—one he'd been quietly introduced to a few minutes before—entered the plane. That was another curious situation, but again, not his concern.

"Is the snow going to be a problem?" Chat asked one of the ground crew.

"For an Otter? Not on your life. One of the safest planes around. Trust me, your boys will get to Fairbanks safe and sound."

But the plane never made it to Fairbanks.

That night, *The Wonder Boys* disappeared. The search went on for weeks to no avail.

The same night the band left for Fairbanks, Chat arrived in Seattle. The next morning, the police informed him of his band's disappearance.

An hour later, Chat Olson slipped out of his hotel.

It was the last anyone ever saw of him.

PART ONE

Chapter 1

ALASKA—PRESENT DAY

"Small adjustments," I said to Michaela.
"I know. I know. My instructor keeps telling me that."
"It might be a good idea to listen to him," I said.
"You're a pain," answered Michaela.

I flashed back to me saying that to my father when he was teaching me to drive. He would tell me to release the clutch slowly, but I would always let it up too fast, and the car would stall. We were practically the only family that didn't own an automatic. My father liked the feel of a standard transmission, so we all had to suffer. As a result, it took me longer to learn to drive than it did my friends. I had a lot more trial and error to deal with.

In this case, though, we were almost 10,000 feet in the air, and a wrong move could present a significant problem.

For the first time, I understood the nervousness my father must have felt as he taught me to drive.

Luckily, I wasn't Michaela's instructor. But I had become somewhat of a surrogate instructor since she always flew with me. She couldn't get her license or fly solo until she was sixteen, but she could take lessons and hone her skills. By sixteen, she'd have a lot of hours of training behind her.

Michaela was thirteen. I had adopted her a couple of months earlier after we found ourselves fighting a common enemy in the middle of the Alaska wilderness. Michaela had no living parents, so it seemed natural that I would adopt her. I was forty, with no kids and no permanent relationship on the horizon. Michaela and I had bonded immediately, and the fact that my best friend, Max, loved her sealed the deal.

Max was a German Shepherd—an ex-police dog I had inherited from his dying handler. Max and I went everywhere together. And now, Max, Michaela, and I went everywhere together.

I noticed though, that Max was looking a little nervous with Michaela at the controls.

"Okay, the lesson is over for the day," I said.

"That was cheap," said Michaela. "I only had the controls for a few minutes."

"Seemed like hours to me," I said.

That got me a punch in the arm.

We were returning from dropping off some supplies to a small town a couple hundred miles from my home base of Homer. My old plane, the Piper Apache, died a violent death at the hands of some nasty people during the same adventure where I discovered Michaela. Meeting Michaela wasn't the only good thing that happened. I also broke up a terrorist group and located a large cache of lost treasure. I came out of it very well, financially, and immediately bought my dream plane—a DeHavilland Canada DHC-2 Beaver. The Beaver had the reputation of being the best "bush" plane ever built. They stopped making them in the 1960s, but refurbished Beavers were still available—at a hefty price! This one had been configured for two pilots instead of the standard single pilot. I had seen a few like that and wanted one specifically so Michaela could take the controls—something my nerves regretted every time she did.

Many of the Beavers in Alaska had been converted to seaplanes, but I wasn't ready to do that. I preferred "real" runways. Of course, that meant I couldn't access some of the more remote hunting and fishing camps on the edges of lakes. But that didn't concern me. I was doing what I wanted and earning a nice income doing it.

The Beaver was larger than my Apache and had room for six passengers in addition to the pilot. It also had a lot of cargo space.

It was getting toward evening. I would land back at Homer in the dark, but I wasn't concerned—it was normal during certain times of the year. It was the end of September, and Michaela had a week off. A water main burst at her school and caused a fair amount of damage. The kids were given the week off while it was being repaired. I was okay with having Michaela home—I liked her company.

She had filled out some since I first met her. She was tall for her age and had been quite skinny and pale. My cooking took care of the skinny part. She was now at a healthy weight. But she was still pale. Maybe she always would be. Her blonde hair didn't help in that department.

I was the opposite. Besides being almost thirty years older, I was … well … chunky. I had lost a lot of weight during our adventure—lack of food and lots of hiking will do that to you—but had gained some of it back. I had a full head of dark hair with flecks of gray and, at the moment, was sporting a full beard. The beard came and went regularly.

We flew in silence for a few minutes. I preferred

conversation at this time of day. Sometimes, I would get a bit tired, and falling asleep wouldn't end well. Before I met Michaela, I would have long, rambling conversations with Max. He wasn't the best conversationalist, but he was a good listener.

"Talk to me," I told Michaela through the headphones—a necessity in a small plane due to the engine's noise.

"Oh my God!" she exclaimed.

Not exactly what I was expecting.

"What?"

"Look!" She turned in her seat and pointed to the horizon behind us.

A reflection had caught her attention, causing her to turn and look. I looked out the window.

"Holy cow!" I exclaimed.

I quickly banked the plane to the right and reversed direction. In front of us was the most magnificent Aurora Borealis I had ever seen.

I had witnessed this phenomenon a few times in the ten years or so I had lived in Alaska, but nothing like this. The blues and greens dominated the sky, making it a magnificent work of art. I was awestruck.

Michaela was snapping picture after picture with her phone.

I continued in that direction for almost five minutes, then decided we had seen enough. It was time to get home. I turned back toward Homer.

A minute later, Michaela said, "What's that?"

I saw it, too. It was a flash in the forest below us, reflecting the painted sky.

I banked again, this time descending as I turned.

"You saw it?" asked Michaela.

"I did. I don't know what it is, but I saw something. It might be as simple as a metal shed, but I don't think so—not way out here."

"There," she said, pointing.

Of course, from a few thousand feet up, she could have been pointing to anything. But I got the gist of it and knew approximately where to look. The Borealis was almost gone, but I caught another glimpse of whatever caught our attention.

I flew as low as I dared. Was that the tail of a plane? If so, it was old—very old. The dusk made it hard to see.

"Mark the location," I said. "I don't have any jobs planned for tomorrow, so we can fly back here if you want."

"I want."

"We're about an hour from home, so it'll be an easy flight. If it's really the tail section of a plane, we can call it in."

"It looked old from here."

"I agree. That's why I'm not calling it in right now."

Was it really an old crash site? And if so, how old was it?

And how did it end up there?

Chapter 2

We slept late the next morning. We were tired from the long day and weren't eager to get out of bed. When I finally got up, I made breakfast. Michaela appeared from her bedroom just as I was about to call her.

"Your knack for showing up just as I've prepared a meal is uncanny," I said.

She grunted.

Michaela wasn't exactly a bright-eyed and bushy-tailed kind of person in the morning.

"Still want to check out the plane?" I asked.

She nodded in response. That was the most enthusiasm she could muster. Michaela ate her eggs in a zombielike fashion, but by the time she was done, she had begun to wake up.

"Do I have time for a shower?" she asked.

"If it'll turn you into a functioning human, you do."

She made a face, letting me know I wasn't funny, then headed into the bathroom.

Were kids always this surly in the morning? Maybe it was just the result of adopting a thirteen-year-old—I hadn't had the chance to mold her from birth. Of course, knowing me, that was probably a good thing.

While Michaela showered, I made some sandwiches and

put them in a cooler to bring with us. When she emerged from the bathroom a half-hour later, she was a new person—awake and ready to go. It's incredible how someone can go from sullen to perky so quickly.

"Ready," she said.

"Then let's go. C'mon, Max."

An hour later, we were in the air, heading northwest over Cook Inlet to Lake Clark National Park and Preserve. It was there that we saw the plane's tail.

Michaela was looking at the map, getting suggestions from Max, who was looking over her shoulder. Of course, most of his suggestions had to do with food.

"I think we're coming close," said Michaela. "It looks different in the daylight, but I think it's around here somewhere."

"It is," I said. "I recognize that ridge over there."

"I see it!" she yelled, pointing. "It's right down there."

And so it was. I descended and circled the area. Trees hid all but the tail, but it looked like it was still attached to the fuselage.

"I think that's an Otter," I said.

"You can see an otter from up here?"

"No, a DeHavilland Otter, a plane similar to my Beaver. I would have heard if an Otter went down, so it must be old like we thought."

"Why wouldn't anyone have seen it before now?"

"They had a bad storm go through here last week. Maybe the wind took away some of the plane's tree cover."

"Do we have to call it in right now?" Michaela asked. "I'd love to look at it first."

"If it's as old as I think it is, I doubt it would make any difference by waiting to call it in. I saw a valley a couple of miles from here. Let's go check it out as a possible landing site."

We memorized the lay of the land, then flew toward the valley I had seen. I flew over it at a low altitude to make sure there weren't any rocks or holes that could damage the plane. As I suspected, it looked conducive to landing.

Ten minutes later, we were on the ground. The landing had been bumpier than I expected, but the plane handled it well.

"I figure we're about two miles from the crash site," I said. "Ready for some walking?"

"Try to keep up."

"Don't go too fast. I'm an old man."

"That's for sure."

I didn't need her to agree with me.

Michaela talked a good talk, but in the end, she stayed with me as we walked. I wasn't worried either way. Max would have watched her if she had gone ahead.

I wasn't worried about my plane either. I couldn't imagine another living soul within miles of where we landed. Over my shoulder was my Winchester '73 rifle, and I also carried a .45 semi-automatic handgun. You never knew what you might encounter out there. Michaela was armed with a 9mm semi-automatic. One might question giving a gun to a 13-year-old, but Michaela knew how to use it and had been forced to shoot a couple of people during our last adventure. I wasn't concerned about her.

The going got tougher once we were beyond the valley and into the woods. The terrain was mountainous, which made for slow progress. We had to scale large hills and skirt rock ledges. There were no trails to speak of, and the ground was anything but flat.

It took us about three hours to reach the crash site. Dense

foliage made the area particularly gloomy, which somehow fit the scene.

I was right. It was an Otter. Actually, a Twin Otter, and about the same vintage as my Beaver. But that's where the comparison ended. This plane had been here a long time. Decades, I guessed. The harsh Alaska weather had taken a toll. The plane was rusted out, and the tail numbers were faded to the point of not being readable.

I was also right about a recent storm opening up the tree cover. A large branch was on the ground, clearly a recent break. Who knows how long it would have been before someone discovered the wreckage if it hadn't broken off?

"Be very careful," I said to Michaela. "There's a lot of sharp, protruding metal. This wouldn't be a good place to get cut."

As a paramedic, I never went anywhere without my medical kit. I had a large kit onboard the plane but had a smaller one that I carried in my backpack. Even so, an accident in the middle of nowhere could prove fatal.

"I'll be careful," said Michaela.

"Max, you stay here," I said. For the same reason, I didn't want Max anywhere near the pieces of the plane strewn all around. Most of the pieces were very rusted, and some were almost completely buried—the result of years of rainstorms.

As we approached the wreckage, I felt goosebumps on my arms. Why did I feel like I was about to enter another age?

"Are you sure you want to go in?" I asked Michaela. "There might be the skeletal remains of the passengers."

"And I haven't seen that before?"

"True. I forgot who I was talking to."

In our adventure together, Michaela saw many freshly killed bodies and a ship full of skeletons. There was nothing here that would surprise her.

But there was something that surprised me.

Chapter 3

We pulled flashlights from our backpacks. Even though it was midday, it was dark in the woods. The only bit of muted sunshine came from the open space in the trees created by the storm. It would be even darker inside the plane.

We didn't have to worry about entering through a door. There was a large hole in the plane's fuselage where the cargo door had once been.

"Be careful," I said for the second time.

"Yup. I heard you the first time." She realized how rude that sounded and quickly added, "But I appreciate your concern."

"Good save," I said.

"I thought so."

Max stood on guard at the edge of the debris area. I didn't worry about being surprised by a large, unfriendly animal waiting for us inside the plane, as Max would have detected it and warned us.

The inside of the plane was a mess. Over the years, many animals had taken shelter there. Piles of animal droppings, both old and new, littered the floor. I heard a crunch as I stepped and shone my flashlight down at my boots to see what I had stepped on. It was what was left of a guitar. It was only the neck and a small piece of the body, which I had crushed with my boot.

"Be careful," said Michaela.

"Funny."

"Oh!" Michaela let out an exclamation and took a step back.

I guess it didn't matter how many skeletons we had seen. It was still a bit of a shock to run across one. Michaela shined her light at a skeleton sitting in a seat with his seatbelt on. I said "his" only because what was left of his clothing appeared to be what a guy would wear.

"Okay, there's one," I said. "Let's see how many more are in here."

From just inside the hole to the outside, we shined our lights around the plane's interior. There were ten seats in two rows along the walls, although many were perched at odd angles from the crash. A few had come away from the floor. Michaela pointed to a corner near the cockpit, where a skeleton lay crumpled against the wall.

"He wasn't wearing his seatbelt," I said.

"Another one over there," said Michaela. That one was still seated but had a piece of metal stuck between his ribs and through the back of his seat.

"Well, we know how he died," I said.

In all, we found the remains of seven passengers—two were in their seats, and the rest were in piles toward the front of the cabin. Many of the bones had teeth marks from the hungry animals that had found them soon after the crash.

"Why are most of them against the front wall?" asked Michaela.

"The force of the crash. They weren't wearing seatbelts and were dead the minute they hit the wall. Any of the bones not against the wall were probably dragged by an animal."

Besides the passengers were the two pilots. The pilot was still strapped in, but the co-pilot was half in the plane and half out, having gone through the windshield. Why wouldn't they both be wearing seatbelts?

"Two pilots and seven passengers," I said. "We'll need to tell the authorities so they can check back on missing flights from the past. Now, let's see if any of these guys have identification."

I tried the first guy we saw—the one with his seatbelt still on. I reached for his back pocket, where he most likely kept his wallet. As I did, his leg broke. I tried to be as gentle as possible to make it easier for the medical examiner, but the bones were so brittle it was difficult.

I reached into his back pockets. Nothing. That made sense. When I was going to be sitting for a long time, I always took out my wallet. Who knows where he might have put it?

Michaela saw the disappointment on my face.

"Maybe one of the piles still has his pants," she suggested.

It was a good suggestion, and since the bones were already broken, I wouldn't make any more work for the ME.

The first pile still had pants, although they were in tatters—probably from animals. Lo and behold, there was a wallet. I opened it and found the driver's license. It was faded, but I could still read it.

"Looks like this crash was from the mid-1960s," I said. "His license was issued in 1965 and was due to be renewed in 1970. So, we have a timeframe. His name is Travis Miller. Do you have a pen and paper?"

Michaela gave me a look that let me know I was an idiot.

"What century are you from?" she asked. "People have phones with apps for taking notes. Surprisingly, the app is usually called *Notes*."

"It's altogether possible that I might leave you in the woods and let you find your way home."

She smirked. Then she pulled out her phone and typed in the name I just gave her.

"Pile of bones number one is Travis Miller," she said.

I shook my head. Leaving her in the woods wasn't such a bad idea.

I found a wallet in the next pile.

"Holt Pearson," I said. She typed it into her phone.

Something clicked in my head. I held the license and just stared at it.

"What?" asked Michaela.

I didn't say anything. My mind was going a hundred miles an hour.

"What?"

"Holy ... shit! Excuse my language."

"Yeah, like I haven't heard it before. What is it?"

"Holt Pearson. If I'm not mistaken, we might find wallets for Arlo Hays and Frankie Dale."

"Wait. You know them?"

"Not personally. I'm not that old. They died before I was born. These guys were members of *The Wonder Boys*, a rock band from the 1960s. They were flying from Anchorage to Fairbanks. Their plane disappeared and was never seen again."

"This isn't anywhere near Fairbanks or Anchorage," said Michaela. "A totally different direction."

"Which is probably why they were never found."

"Who was Travis Miller?"

"Probably one of their roadies. If I remember the story, it was the three band members and three roadies."

"But there are seven remains."

"So, I got the story wrong. It was especially weird that their manager wasn't on board, but he disappeared the next day and has never been found."

"How do you know this?"

"It's rock legend. It's like Buddy Holly, Ritchie Valens, and the others dying in a plane crash in the 1950s."

"Never heard of them."

"Doesn't matter. Trust me. This is big."

"Uh, Scott?"

Michaela's voice had taken on a different tone.

"Yeah?"

"Look at this."

She stood next to the man with the metal through his bones and pointed to something on the floor.

"I don't think this is supposed to be here."

I stepped over to where she was and shined my light on the floor.

A shell casing.

"Whoa," I said. "What's that doing here?"

Michaela was shining her light all around.

"Another one … and another one."

We counted four altogether.

We looked at each other. The casings were old. These had been here since the plane went down.

"Don't touch anything," I said.

"Don't worry. I'm not."

I moved back to the man we had first encountered and shined my light up and down his body. There it was, a tiny hole in the back of the seat. I set down my backpack and pulled out my medical kit.

"You're too late," said Michaela. "I think he's dead."

"Funny."

I pulled out some tweezers.

"Shine your light on the hole," I said.

I reached around the skeleton with my left hand to widen the hole's opening, then went through some missing ribs with the hand holding the tweezers.

"I know I said not to touch anything, but I have to see if my theory is right."

"I think it will be," said Michaela, holding the light with a slightly trembling hand.

It only took a minute to find it. Using the tweezers, I pulled out a bullet. I put it in a small plastic bag I kept in the kit.

"Let's check the others."

The man with the metal through him had a small hole in his skull. A skull in one of the piles also had a hole. That told me that these men were shot before the plane crashed. None of the others had bullet holes in their skulls. Assuming the others were also shot, they were probably body shots—the heart, most likely.

"Whoa," I said again.

Suddenly, this was a lot bigger than just a plane crash!

Chapter 4

It was time to go.

We found the wallet for Arlo Hays but not any of the others. I wasn't surprised, considering the age of the crash and the state of the remains. I considered us lucky to have found the second band member. There was no doubt now who we were looking at.

The question was, *what* were we looking at?

It wasn't a simple plane crash.

I took pictures of the driver's licenses, put them back in the wallets, and then set the wallets back with the correct remains. I put the bag with the bullet in my medical kit. We took a lot more pictures of the skeletons, the shell casings, and the general state of the mess, then headed back to my plane. It was already getting dark, even though it was only mid-afternoon. It was hard enough walking in the light. This was going to take us longer.

On the way back, I told Michaela what I remembered about *The Wonder Boys*.

"I know some of their songs, though they weren't my cup of tea. But in their time, they were big and had a lot of hits. I read an article about them once that said that with the British Invasion, their popularity was destined to be short-lived."

"Wait." Michaela stopped in her tracks. "The British invaded us?"

I stopped and looked at her.

"You're joking, right?" she asked.

"That's what I was going to ask you," I replied. "No, the British didn't invade us."

I shook my head and started walking.

"Then what do you mean?"

"Ever hear of the Beatles?"

"Of course."

"The Rolling Stones?"

"Yes."

"The Who?"

I was expecting it to lead into an Abbott and Costello routine. But luckily, it didn't.

"Nope."

"Herman's Hermits?"

"No, but I like the name."

"These were all bands that came over from the UK. There were many others, too. They totally changed rock music. Because they all seemed to come over around the same time, they were called the British Invasion."

"Got it. And what's the story with the plane crash?"

"I don't really know. Remember, it was before my time. All I know is what I told you—they were supposed to go from Anchorage to Fairbanks, and just disappeared."

"I'll have to read up on it," she said.

"You do that, then let me know what you find."

"You could read up on it, too, you know."

"No, I like it better this way. You do the work, then report back."

This was the basis of our outer relationship—friendly

banter. Michaela was super-intelligent for her age, which allowed us to get into some pretty good discussions. But that was just the surface. The foundation of our relationship was a deep love and respect that had developed early on. I couldn't imagine my life without my newly found daughter.

"Of course," I said, "whatever you find online won't have anything about bullets and murder."

The return trip to the plane didn't take us as long as I thought it would, but by the time we reached the valley where the plane was, dusk had set in. We walked the path that would serve as our runway, just to make sure there weren't any hidden holes or boulders that I missed when we landed. Everything looked pretty smooth, so I was confident we wouldn't run into any problems taking off.

As we approached the plane, Max let out a quiet growl.

"What is it, boy?" I asked, quickly taking the Winchester from my shoulder. Michaela took her gun out.

We looked at each other with puzzled expressions. The chances of another person being out here were slim, so it had to be an animal. And yet, Max wasn't reacting the way he did when he sensed a bear or moose. He was sniffing the ground but kept looking toward the plane. When we were a few yards away, he seemed to calm down. Maybe an animal had been there checking out the plane and had left.

Still, I opened the door warily. I didn't even have to say anything to Max—he jumped in ahead of me and began sniffing everything. I stuck my head in and sniffed. Hey, if he could do it, so could I.

There was a faint odor of unwashed body and an even fainter smell of cigarettes.

Someone had been in my plane!

Chapter 5

"What is it?" asked Michaela from outside.

"We've had a visitor," I answered. "A human one."

I told Max to go out and stay near Michaela while I searched the plane. I didn't want anyone to snatch Michaela while I was busy. Whoever had been there had gone through my papers but had taken nothing—at least nothing that I was aware of. I checked my big medical kit—nothing missing. Then I looked in the storage locker. Everything seemed to be there.

No, not everything. I had a box of .45 ammunition. It was no longer in the storage locker.

I called out to Michaela, "I had a box of .45s in here, right?"

"Yes. I saw it this morning when I was stowing my sweatshirt."

"It's not here now. We need to leave. Get in."

And then I felt my skin crawl. I was wrong. There was something else missing.

"Faster," I said. "We need to get out of here."

Max climbed in, followed by Michaela. Within minutes, we were rumbling down our makeshift runway, then began our ascent. It was more than just a creepy person having been in my plane. Now I was worried. I didn't reveal that to Michaela, but I didn't need to—she already knew.

"What's wrong?" she asked. "The person stole something else, didn't they?"

"They did. I didn't even notice it at first. They stole the plane's registration. That has all my information on it. Why would they want that?"

I tried to put it out of my mind and concentrate on the next step—informing the authorities about the discovery. But who? Probably the FBI made the most sense. After our last adventure, I had developed a friendly relationship with an agent in the Anchorage office.

The flight to Homer was routine. I let Michaela pilot us for a few minutes, and then, much to Max's relief, I took over again. We landed in the late afternoon, and I immediately called my contact at the FBI.

Special Agent Briggs had come to Alaska after solving a large smuggling ring in the Caribbean. Briggs was a highly decorated agent who could have had any assignment he wanted. Oddly, he chose Anchorage—usually a wasteland for agents. He had come up to work on the incident Michaela and I were involved in and decided that he loved the area. The Caribbean's loss was Alaska's gain. He hadn't experienced an Alaska winter yet; so the jury was still out on how soon before he'd request a transfer. We didn't meet him until our exploits in the wilderness were over—he was the agent assigned to debrief us. During that time, we got to know him pretty well.

I dialed and he answered on the second ring.

"Briggs."

"Special Agent Briggs, this is Scott Harper."

"Hey, how are you doing?"

"Good. I have…"

"And Michaela?"

"She's good. Look, I…"

"Most importantly, how's Max?"

"I'll send him up to bite you if you don't let me tell you why I called."

"So, you're not calling to ask me to join you for a beer?"

"No."

"Okay then, what do you have for me?"

"The Wonder Boys."

"Say again?"

"I have the location of the plane that went down with the band *The Wonder Boys* in the sixties."

I heard him pull his chair in.

"No shit?" His voice had taken on a serious tone.

"No shit. Michaela, Max, and I discovered it today. There was a place to land a couple of miles away, and we walked to the crash site. We checked it out—touching things as little as possible, I might add—and found the bones of seven passengers and two pilots. We also found three wallets. One belonged to Holt Pearson, one to Arlo Hays, and one to someone named Travis Miller, who must have been one of the roadies. I took pictures of their licenses. I'll text them to you when we hang up. I have a lot of other pictures of the scene that I'll text you, too."

"This is amazing! Where did you find them?"

"Nowhere near where they were supposed to be," I said. I gave him the location.

"That explains why none of the searchers ever discovered them," said Briggs.

"Exactly."

"This is fantastic!" he shouted. The man was most definitely excited. "I'll be down in the morning on a chopper. Can you take us there?"

"Of course."

"That place you set down. Anything closer to the crash site than that?"

"Why? Are you too lazy to walk? I'm just kidding. No, it's pretty dense forest all around."

"That's too bad," said Briggs. "Well, we have a start. I'll let the NTSB figure out the logistics. Wait a minute. You said there were seven passengers?" I heard him typing on his computer. "According to reports from the time…"

"I know. There were three band members and three roadies besides the pilot and co-pilot," I said. "It's all part of the folklore."

"Exactly. Are you sure about the number?"

"Positive."

"Well, that will change the history books. Maybe one of the band members snuck a woman on board."

"I don't think so. Based on the clothing remnants, I'm guessing they were all male."

"Okay, so someone snuck a man on board. Doesn't matter. I'm sure they'll figure out who it is from the DNA."

"Uh, Briggs, there's something else."

"Oh?"

"The plane crash didn't kill them."

"You mean they lived through the crash?"

"No. The opposite. They were dead before the crash."

"How could you possibly know that?"

"The shell casings on the floor were a clue. The small holes in the skulls of a couple of them were another clue. And the bullet I pulled out of the seat behind one of the dead guys kind of confirmed it. So, I take back what I said. Besides the driver's licenses, I did touch one item, but only with tweezers. I'll text you a picture of it, then give you the bullet tomorrow."

"Well, that changes things," he said quietly.

"One more thing," I said. "Can you keep my name out of it? I hate reporters."

"I get it. I'll do my best."

After we hung up, I called my brother, Jon, who lived with his wife, Jess, in a house on some property I owned. I invited them over to hear the news. Now that the colder weather was setting in, they'd be leaving soon to winter in Hawaii.

Jon and Jess were instrumental in solving the Wisdom Spring affair a while back, which would've had devastating worldwide implications if it hadn't been stopped. I came to their aid at the time. In return, they helped me out when I was dealing with the terrorists deep in the heart of Alaska.

Jon was my older brother by a couple of years. Growing up, he was the steady one, while I was the wild brother. I was always skirting the law and getting in trouble, but he was always there for me. When I got my act together and became a paramedic, I began to worry about him. He had a high-level sales job and brought in a big salary. He had a beautiful young daughter he was devoted to and a wife I disliked from the beginning. Long story short, his daughter died, his wife divorced him, and he was about to go over the edge. But that's when he found Jess and got involved in the Wisdom Spring conspiracy. Jess and the conspiracy, as dangerous as it was, saved his life. They wrote a book about it afterward and secured a seven-figure advance, allowing them to live half the year in Alaska and the other half in Hawaii.

I couldn't wait to tell them about the discovery of *The Wonder Boys*.

And, if he was up to it, I could use Jon's help.

I wanted to find out who had been in my plane and stole my registration!

*****

Jon and Jess came by for dinner. It was funny how they always managed to arrive at dinnertime. I mentioned that to them when they walked in.

"It's your fault for being a good cook," said Jon. "We like your food."

"What Jon is trying to say is that our cooking sucks," said Jess.

Jess was around thirty—a lot younger than Jon—and almost a foot shorter. She barely topped five feet. She was blonde—at least today. She was known for changing her hair color, but she said that blonde was her natural color. I'd have to take her at her word for that.

During dinner, I told them the news about finding the crash site.

"Wow," said Jon. "That is a major find. And just what you want—more publicity."

"I talked to Briggs, and he said he'd try to keep my name out of it, but I don't have great hopes."

After dinner, Jon and I took a walk outside. Jess and Michaela didn't even notice. They had become almost inseparable since I adopted Michaela. It was good for Michaela to have a female role model—and there was none better than Jess.

"You want my help for something," said Jon as we walked up a familiar trail, flashlights in hand. Jon was a couple of inches taller than me. He was clean-cut, a lot thinner than me, with short brown hair. He hadn't yet adopted the "Alaska look."

"I do."

I told him about the visitor to the plane.

"I need to get the registration back or at least know why they stole it. It's important. I need to find this person, but I don't know if they are dangerous."

"Danger seems to have become commonplace for us these days," said Jon. "Of course, I'll help you. That goes without saying."

"Thank you. I have to show Briggs the crash site tomorrow, so maybe the next day? And who knows? Maybe we'll come across the person tomorrow, and you and I won't have to worry about it."

Somehow, though, I knew that wouldn't be the case.

Chapter 6

An FBI helicopter landed at Homer Airport early the next morning, and Michaela and I were there to greet it. Sadly, I had to leave Max home, as Briggs informed me that they would have a full load and no room for Max. I think Briggs was as sad as I was.

Max seemed okay about it, though. When we left, he was napping.

Briggs exited the chopper with his head down. That was a natural reaction to having blades spinning above your head, but unless you were freakishly tall, the chances of your head being lopped off were pretty slim.

We shook hands.

"Good to see you, Scott."

"You, too, Briggs."

It's funny that he called me by my first name, and I called him by his last name. It occurred to me that I didn't even know his first name—unless it was "Special Agent."

Briggs gave Michaela a hug. I think it kind of surprised her. It didn't surprise me. I remember Briggs being impressed by Michaela's maturity and the stories of her calmness under fire. He took an immediate liking to her and was especially happy when he heard I had adopted her. In some ways, I think Briggs kind of envied me. We were alike in that we were both loners. I think he would have liked someone in his life, even if it were a child, like Michaela.

"You ready to go?" he asked.

"Ready."

He saw that Michaela and I both had holsters with handguns.

"Um, is that really necessary?" he asked.

I told him about the visitor I'd had to my plane.

"Besides," I added, "we'll be in the wilds of Alaska. You never go unprepared. If there had been room, I would have brought my rifle."

Once we were strapped in, the helicopter took off, and I gave the pilot the coordinates. The chopper was large, but all the seats were taken by a hodgepodge of FBI agents, NTSB people, and forensic types. There were a dozen of us altogether, not including the pilot and co-pilot.

The helicopter was fast, and we arrived over the crash site about an hour after taking off. An FBI agent and two NTSB people were winched down to the plane to get a head start on the process. The rest of us would have to walk from the valley.

When we landed and stepped down from the helicopter, I couldn't help thinking that we were being watched. I didn't want to say anything to Briggs since it was just a feeling. Besides, I didn't want him to think that I was a wimp. But because the pilots were staying behind, I felt it was an obligation. Briggs took the news in stride, and both pilots had guns on them.

Michaela and I led the way across the rough terrain. I had to give the others credit—they all seemed experienced in the Alaska bush, even Briggs, the newcomer.

"We'll have to do something about this," he said as we

approached the site. "We can't expect our people to hike here from the valley. We might have to clear out an area for a chopper to land. But that's up to the NTSB. They are in charge at a crash site."

When we arrived, there were many exclamations of surprise and looks of excitement. After all, they were there at a moment in history, about to solve an almost 60-year-old mystery. They were all taking pictures with their personal phones. I'm sure that wasn't technically allowed, but this was a special moment. Nobody was going to report them.

The people we had dropped in earlier had secured the area around the crash with crime scene tape. I wasn't sure how necessary that was. There were no people out here—except maybe the one who had been in my plane—and bears and moose weren't known for their reading prowess. But I guess they had to follow procedure. As for clearing out some of the trees, they had already called for another helicopter to deliver some tree people to cut down trees and clear away brush about ten yards from the plane to give them a place to work and another, much larger, space about fifty yards away for use as a landing pad.

Michaela and I had nothing to do. Our job was to show them where it was, so it quickly became boring for us. All we could do was stand around and watch.

Things got loud when the other helicopter arrived with the tree workers, who immediately got to work. The sound of chainsaws seemed out of place in the tranquil woods.

To our relief, by early afternoon, Briggs was ready to leave. The tree cutters were making significant progress and would soon have a space for a helicopter to land to bring more forensic people and to be able to transport the remains out of there.

Five other FBI agents joined us as we trekked back to the helicopter.

"This is huge," said Briggs. "I'm told that the media already has the story."

"Which means an influx of reporters," I sighed.

"There's no reason for them to travel to your neck of the woods. They'll all be based in Anchorage," said Briggs, "and we'll limit their access to the site. The nice thing for you is that your job is done."

Yeah, if I could believe that.

Chapter 7

SEATTLE, WASHINGTON—1966

Chat looked in disbelief at the police officer who had told him about *The Wonder Boys'* disappearance.

It couldn't be! The man at the airport said the Otter was the safest plane around and that the weather wouldn't be a problem.

If it wasn't the weather or the plane, it had to do with the man behind the concert. Or maybe it was the man Chat had secretly let aboard the aircraft. The coincidences were too obvious, especially if he connected them to what he heard in the airport bathroom back in Anchorage after the plane with his band had taken off.

*****

Chat closed the door to the bathroom stall and wiped down the toilet seat.

"Pigs," he muttered.

Once it was clean, he sat down on the seat. Chat didn't really have to use the bathroom. He just often found it to be a peaceful location to think. This particular bathroom was in a quiet area of the terminal at the Anchorage airport. He sat back and put his feet up against the door.

Yeah, it was a strange habit, but it brought him comfort. If he'd had a pillow behind his back, it would have been perfect. He might have even been able to nap.

He'd had second thoughts about leaving the children on their own. But frankly, he was tired of them. He was tired of the whole music business. He didn't like all the travel, and he hated babysitting morons. The money was good, and he had already stockpiled enough to live on for a long time. But the money was the only good part about it. It was time to say goodbye to this life.

He would tell the band when they arrived in Seattle.

Chat decided not to accompany the band to Fairbanks for three reasons. First, he was sick of the cold. How could anyone call Alaska home? He needed warm weather and a nice warm hotel room. The second reason was obvious—he needed to separate himself from those idiots for a while. He needed a temporary break from them before telling them that he'd be taking a permanent break from them.

The third reason was the most important one. He didn't feel right about the trip. The bigwig his promoter asked him to do the favor for was scary. He was from Russia or one of those Eastern European countries. He had a deep voice—the kind that commanded respect. More accurately, the kind that let you know that if you didn't show him respect, you would regret it in a painful manner.

And then there was Travis Miller. He had hired him because Steve Brown, one of their regular roadies, disappeared. That was unlike Steve, but there wasn't anything Chat could do about it. He needed to find a replacement fast. Travis Miller appeared out of the blue and seemed to know exactly what to do, so Chat hired him. Now, he was suspicious of the man. When they met the large Russian—or whatever he was—there was a look between him and Travis Miller. Did they know one another?

There was another thing. Chat thought the concert in Fairbanks was for the big man, but then he heard that the man was catching a flight to Montreal, not Fairbanks. If so, why did they need a concert in Fairbanks?

There were just too many questions that he didn't have answers to.

The door to the bathroom opened, and he saw two pairs of feet go past the stall.

"Is it empty?"

He knew that voice. The scary Russian!

Chat didn't move. He saw the other man go down on one knee. He must've been looking for feet, but Chat's were in the air against the door.

"It's empty," said the other man. It was the promoter. His name was Dickson.

Chat couldn't move now. He didn't know why, but he was suddenly afraid for his life.

"Is he on the flight?" asked the Russian.

"He is," answered the promoter.

"Does he know his job?"

"Of course."

"Be careful how you talk to me," said the Russian threateningly.

"I'm sorry. But please understand that everything is fine. It'll go smoothly. The pilots know where to go."

"And our man?" asked the Russian.

"He knows, too, but the pilots will handle the situation."

"Good. The fewer people who know, the better."

"We might have one small problem, but nothing we can't take care of quickly—Olson."

Chat stiffened, and his legs almost slipped off the door.

"What about him," asked the Russian.

"He's not on the flight."

"Where is he?"

"I heard he's going to Seattle and plans to meet the band there."

"Is he a problem?"

"I don't think so," answered the promoter.

"Then don't worry about it. We'll see how it goes."

The two men left the bathroom. Chat sat there, almost paralyzed. Were they intimating what he thought they were? And who were they talking about as being on the flight? Was it Travis Miller? It had to be. It couldn't have been the man Chat let on the flight. That man was too official.

Chat sat there for ten more minutes. During that time, several more men came in, used the facilities, and left. Finally, he felt that it was safe to leave. By now, his legs were cramping. He stood up and slowly opened the stall door. He knew the promoter and the Russian man were gone, but he was cautious anyway. When he opened the door to the bathroom, he looked up and down the hallway, but it was empty.

Then he headed for his flight to Seattle.

*****

He had been looking forward to a couple of days without the children, as he called them. Frankly, they exhausted him. Was he that immature twenty years ago when he was their age? He sure hoped not. Part of it was their maturity level, and part of it was their stupidity. It was like they had never gone to school. Even Holt, who wrote some of the finest songs Chat had ever heard, was otherwise an idiot. Maybe he was some kind of musical savant.

Yes, a night or two without them was heaven. He had looked up an old girlfriend who just happened to be single again after the end of a bad marriage. They had a romantic dinner at a quiet restaurant, reliving old times. One thing led to another, and they spent the night together at Chat's hotel.

It was a wonderful night and a needed diversion from the stress of managing the children.

Until the knock on the door.

He thanked the police officer and shut the door, leaning against it to catch his breath. They were missing, but he knew in his gut that they were dead. Was it his fault? He thought back to the Russian with the deep voice. Could the conversation he overheard have something to do with it?

And the other man—the man who introduced himself as CIA. The one he let onto the plane at the last minute. Was he really CIA? His ID looked genuine. Did that have something to do with it?

He had to go—now! But where? Anywhere remote. To stay where he was would be suicide. The Russian knew he didn't go with the band on the plane. If he had something to do with it, would he come after Chat next?

"Chat? What's wrong?"

He'd almost forgotten that Nancy was there. She came out of the bathroom with a towel wrapped around her head.

Chat had slumped down to a sitting position.

"Nancy, I've gotta go. I'm sorry. I had a great time last night but can't stay here."

He stood up and hurriedly put on his clothes.

"I don't understand," said Nancy.

What could he tell her? The truth was best—well, part of it.

"My band. Their plane disappeared. No one knows what happened to them."

He didn't have to tell her the other part—the more important part. It was the part of the equation that he didn't understand. He just knew that he had to go. His life depended on it.

"Oh, God! I'm so sorry. Is there anything I can do?"

"Yes, you can. If anyone asks, tell them that I went back to LA."

Of course, he wasn't going to LA, but since his office was there, it was the logical assumption.

"I'm sorry this happened," said Nancy. "When it's all over, will you come back and visit? I felt like we rekindled an old spark last night."

"I did, too."

And he really did. Before the police came, he was going to suggest to her that they see each other more regularly, with all possibilities open to them. He couldn't say that now. At best, the chances that he'd ever see her again were slim.

"As soon as I can, I'll call you," he said. "This is not how I wanted this time with you to end."

He held her close, and they kissed. It was a deep, passionate kiss, and one that Chat wished he could repeat again and again over the years. But he couldn't.

His bag was packed.

"Are you okay leaving on your own?" he asked. "I'll pay the bill on my way out. You've got the room until eleven."

"I'll be fine. You go."

"Okay." He gave her another kiss. "I love you."

She gasped.

"You do?"

"I guess I do."

Did he? Maybe. Or maybe it was just a wish he knew would never happen.

Chat left the room, paid the bill on the way out, and caught a taxi.

"Where to?" asked the cabbie.

And that was the question.

Where was he going?

Chapter 8

PRESENT DAY

Michaela's school fixed their flooding problem, so it was with great reluctance that Michaela got out of the truck the next morning when I dropped her off. She knew she couldn't win any arguments with me about staying home, so she didn't even try. I kissed her and told her to have a good day.

I was glad Michaela had school because I didn't want her around for what Jon and I needed to do. She had already been put in too many dangerous situations. She needed to live a more normal life. Although, I had no idea what a "normal life" for her meant. All I could do was provide her with a loving environment. Hopefully, everything else would take care of itself.

At thirteen, she already knew what she wanted to do in life. She had taken a great interest in archeology, especially after we found the ancient ship in the desert. We had met a half dozen well-known archeologists who had all given her their cards and told her to look them up after high school. I saw a bright future for her.

However, as right as the decision was to adopt Michaela, and as great as our relationship was, it hadn't all been smooth sailing. Michaela missed her mother deeply and had a lot of tearful moments—sometimes while she was with me, sometimes with Jess, but usually when she was alone. There were many times when I heard her crying in her bedroom. I learned quickly to let her have the privacy to mourn. If she wanted to talk about her mother with me—and those times did happen—she knew she always could.

Michaela's mother died of cancer, something no 13-year-old should ever have to witness. She and her mother had been close, which made it all harder. Michaela's father was an evil man who had very little contact with her until the courts forced him to take her after the death of her mother. That's how she ended up in the middle of nowhere—where I met her—while her father put together his nasty plan to kill a lot of people.

I knew she loved living with me and often said how happy her mother would've been that she had ended up here, but it still wasn't easy for her.

It wasn't all fun and games for me, either. I had spent my whole adult life living alone—and I liked it that way, especially since I had never found the right woman to spend it with. Having an instant family took a lot of getting used to. I knew nothing about how to raise a teenager—especially a girl.

So, it was a lot of trial and error for both of us. But we promised each other that we would always talk things through if there was a problem.

*****

Jon met me at the airport. He was armed, which was good. I had no idea what we would find when we got to the landing strip in the valley, and we were both experienced at fighting for our lives ... unfortunately.

Once we were in the air, Jon said, "What exactly are we looking for?"

"This is a fine time to ask, now that you're committed," I laughed. "The truth is, I'm not exactly sure. We're looking for a person, but I don't know who. All I know is that he—or she—broke into my plane and stole my registration and a box of ammo. If it were just the ammo, I wouldn't care. I would chalk it up to someone living in the forest who could use some ammunition. But the registration is troubling. To steal my registration, it means they wanted to know who I was. That's not just some hermit in the woods."

I had brought Max with us, but a part of me regretted that. I always feared for Max in dangerous situations, even though he had spent most of his life fighting bad guys. Well, I was sure he would handle himself as he always did, and he might just help us find the guy.

"Is this a shot in the dark?" asked Jon.

"How did you guess? We're going to land in a narrow valley surrounded by forest. I don't know where the person came from. I don't know if they were passing through and saw the plane, camping nearby and saw it land, or if they have a house nearby. I don't know if the person has a gun—and if so, whether they'd use it. They probably do, since they stole my ammo."

"What you are trying to tell me," said Jon, "is that you are totally clueless."

"Yeah, pretty much."

"I've been saying that about you for years."

"Well, now you'll see it in action."

We spent the rest of the trip lost in our thoughts. Every once in a while, Max would chime in with a little whine to let us know he was still there. It might have been the most intelligent thing any of us said the entire trip.

We landed mid-morning. A couple of miles away, the NTSB was working. Eventually, they would remove everything from the site and take it to a hangar someplace to recreate the scene. There was no need for us to go over there, and now that they had a helicopter pad, no reason for them to be here. It was just Jon, Max, and me. Jess often referred to us as The Three Stooges.

We hopped out of the plane with a rifle and pistol each, but somehow felt that Max was better prepared than the two of us put together.

"Which way do you want to go?" asked Jon. "I feel like a sitting duck out here."

"I know what you mean. Which way, Max?"

I expected him to ask, "How should I know?"

But he didn't.

Instead, he started walking north, toward the trees about thirty yards away. He either figured he knew where he was going or was faking it to keep up an image.

Or the third option. He reached the trees before us and raised his leg to relieve himself.

It turned out to be a good decision.

Jon and I were only about ten yards from the trees when a piece of bark flew off a tree, and a shot rang out less than a second later. We covered the ten yards in record time. Max had disappeared into the forest.

Another shot ... and another. Then they stopped.

"Okay then," Jon said under his breath.

"I guess it wasn't just some curious guy going through the plane," I said.

"Whoever it is doesn't want us here," replied Jon.

"Glad we followed Max," I said. "If we'd chosen the other way, we would have walked right into it. This gives us a chance to go after the shooter through the trees."

"One shooter, you think?" Jon asked.

"Those were all from the same gun," I said. "But it doesn't mean he's alone."

Max poked his head out through some bushes.

"Nice of you to show up," I said. "Now go get the shooter but go through the trees."

I pointed the way I wanted him to go, but it was unnecessary—that was already his plan. He knew there was a bad guy out there and that it was his job to root him out. He took off, body low to the ground, silently weaving in and out of the trees.

"I guess we better follow him," I said to Jon.

We weren't as fast or silent as Max, but we made good time, keeping far enough into the trees to not be seen.

It would take a while to work our way to the other side of the valley, but we had no choice. I had to know what this person was up to. I just hoped that while we were circling, the shooter wasn't also circling, which would land us in the exact same position as before, except on opposite sides.

Twenty minutes later, we were on the other side, creeping slowly through the trees toward the area where we thought the shooter might be. I hadn't heard anything from Max. I hoped that was a good sign.

Suddenly, I heard a high-pitched scream and then a gunshot. It wasn't far ahead of us.

Keeping low, Jon and I raced through the forest. There were sounds of a struggle, and I heard Max at work. His victim was crying out in pain.

We came around a tree, and there they were. Max was

clutching the arm of …

A woman!

That was the last thing I would have suspected. However, this woman wasn't an innocent bystander. A high-powered rifle lay on the ground, and the woman was dressed in military fatigues. But I had a feeling she wasn't military.

She also wasn't innocent, and she wasn't a backwoods mountain woman. She was there with a purpose.

"Okay, Max. Thank you."

He backed off, but he was staring at the woman. There was no doubt that Max meant business.

She sat up and leaned against a tree, holding her arm and staring daggers at me.

"Why were you shooting at us?" I asked.

Silence

"I'm going to search you for an I.D.," I said. "You so much as move a muscle, and I'll have Max rip off your face. Got it?"

"Search all you want," she said. "I have no I.D. on me."

I searched anyway and found nothing. What I did notice was that she was in excellent physical condition. It wasn't like I was trying to feel her up or anything, but there are certain things you notice when doing a search like that. This woman wasn't someone you wanted to mess with—with or without weapons.

"What are you doing here?" I asked.

"None of your business, Scott Harper."

She was the one who stole my registration, and she said my name purposely. She wanted me to know that she knew who I was.

"I want my registration back."

"I don't have it."

Uh oh. That meant there might be others.

"Why are you here?" I asked again.

"I already told you—none of your business."

"Are you here because of the plane crash?"

"I know nothing about a plane crash, but that explains all the Feds you brought on the helicopter. How many times do I have to tell you that what I'm doing here is none of your business?"

"I can have the FBI here in no time. Then we'll find out some answers."

"That wouldn't go well for you," she said, "or for your young friend."

She meant Michaela.

"What the fuck do you mean?" I almost snarled it.

"I'll let you fly out of here..."

"You'll let us?" said Jon.

She ignored him. Then I heard rustling in forest. Max growled.

"I'll let you fly out of here with the understanding that you won't tell anyone that you saw me—that you'll forget you were even here."

I looked at Jon. What was going on here? She obviously felt that she was in a position of power.

And then I found out why.

Stepping out of the trees were three very dangerous-looking men. They were all dressed in the same fatigues as the woman. And they were each pointing large pistols our way.

I stepped back, and the woman stood.

"We're not going to kill you," she said. "Too many people, including your FBI friends, know where to look for you. But I will ask you politely to forget you ever saw us. Why we're here has nothing to do with anything you'd be interested in. I'm asking you nicely, but you can tell that we mean business."

She picked up her rifle and pointed at me for effect.

The effect worked.

"If you don't want to kill us, why were you shooting at us?" I asked.

"To scare you away. If I were trying to kill you, you'd be dead."

"How do you know we won't go straight to the FBI?"

"Without actually killing you, there's only one way to keep you quiet."

I knew what was coming.

"If you tell anyone about this, your little girl will suffer."

Chapter 9

"I suggest you get in your plane and leave before we change our minds," said the woman. "And don't think about getting the girl to someplace safe. We have someone watching her."

I looked at Jon, who shrugged. They had us over a barrel. They knew it, and we knew it.

"I guess we have no choice," I said to her.

"I guess you don't. And you're lucky I don't kill your dog."

None of the men had said a word. It was clear that she was in charge.

"If you killed Max, you'd have to kill us, and then you'd be up shit's creek. You'd have exactly what you don't want—the Feds crawling all over this place. We'll fly out of here and not tell a soul, but only if Max leaves with us."

She nodded.

As we walked back to the plane, I tried to be manly and not look behind me. It didn't work so well. I took a few quick glances. They didn't appear to be ready to shoot us in the back. Their guns were pointing down, and the woman was rubbing her sore wrist. I'm glad Max left her with something to remember him by.

We got in the plane, and I quickly got us up in the air.

"Shit!" said Jon, breathing out. Like me, he'd been holding

his breath.

"You could say that. What do you think it's all about?"

"Terrorists come to mind," said Jon, "but that could mean anything—foreign, home-grown, or whatever other kinds there are. She wasn't foreign, though. Definitely an American accent."

"I thought I was all done with terrorists," I said. "Do I have a sign on me inviting them into my life?"

"Maybe. It sounded to me like they didn't know about the old plane crash, meaning they are here for something totally different."

"I agree."

"So," began Jon, "are you going to tell anyone?"

"Of course I am."

"Good boy."

"We don't know what they are planning. A lot of people could die if we don't tell the Feds. However," I added, "I'll start with Agent Briggs. Meanwhile, we'll figure out a way to sneak Michaela to a safe spot. Do you really think they are watching Michaela?"

"I don't know, but I'd say no. She said, 'We have someone watching.' Why would they have someone watching? They didn't even know we were coming back."

"True," I said.

But it didn't make me feel any better about what they could do to Michaela. After all, maybe the woman meant to say that they could get someone to watch Michaela. Either way, it was scary.

Jon was silent. I could tell he was working something out in his head.

Finally, he said, "Whatever it is, they're not planning on being there very long."

"Why do you say that?" I asked.

"Think about it. If they were setting up something permanent or even semi-permanent, they wouldn't take the chance of us keeping silent. They would do away with us and figure out a way to hide the plane or fly it out of there. In fact, their best bet would be to fly it out of there with us aboard and crash it someplace far from here after bailing out. But that's too much work if they are not planning to stay."

"So, what's your theory?" I asked.

"I haven't a clue. I think we can eliminate anything that would require time, such as human trafficking or drug production and distribution. Even the kind of operation that was going on when you found Michaela."

"So," I began, continuing the thought, "they don't expect to be here very long. They weren't dressed like people setting up camp. Maybe they're looking for something and expect to find it and be gone."

"That's a possibility," said Jon. "We know they weren't looking for the crash site of *The Wonder Boys*, so what else could they be looking for?"

"And, if they weren't using the valley I landed in, how did they get there?"

"Maybe there's another valley or field in a different direction, and they have a plane there," Jon suggested.

"Very possibly. I'll call Briggs when we land and fill him in. Then, we'll have to keep a close eye on Michaela."

*****

As soon as we landed back in Homer, I called Briggs. I let him know about the woman and her friends and told him of their threats against Michaela.

"Scott, you won't want to hear this, but there isn't much I can do."

"What? Why not?"

"Well, they haven't kidnapped anyone, and you don't know for sure that they are terrorists."

"But..."

"You didn't come across any kind of camp, right?"

"No, but..."

"Which means they could be doing something as simple as poaching. You said they had high-powered rifles, right?"

"Yeah."

"Then my guess would be poaching. That falls under the purview of the National Park Service or the local authorities.

"What local authorities?" I asked incredulously. "It's out in the middle of friggin' nowhere."

"My point exactly. It's out in the middle of nowhere for us, too. Scott, I sympathize, and if anything ever happened to Michaela, I'd burn the place down in my efforts to find her. But there just isn't enough to go on. My boss would never approve such an operation."

I didn't like what he had to say, but I also couldn't dispute it.

"If I had to guess," continued Briggs, "I'd still put my money on poachers. They used the threat against Michaela to keep you quiet. Like Jon said, I seriously doubt they have anyone watching her. They probably needed a few more days to finish whatever they were doing. Hey, I'm an animal lover. If they're poaching, I'd like to see them dead. String 'em up and gut them. But we don't have enough information. All I can tell you is to keep an eye on Michaela and don't go back up that way."

"Okay. I don't like it, but you make sense," I said.

"There's something else." His voice dropped to a whisper. "I shouldn't be telling you this, but we're no longer involved in the crash site of *The Wonder Boys*."

"Yeah, you said the NTSB was taking over."

"They're in charge of the physical crash, but everything else is now classified. We no longer have access to any information. We've basically been told to go pound sand."

"By whom?"

"The CIA."

"The CIA? I thought they worked on foreign soil. Last I knew, Alaska was part of the U.S."

"Evidently, this wasn't just a crash."

"What was it?"

"Something so big, they don't even want *us* involved."

He lowered his voice even more.

"Whatever it is, it's huge!"

Chapter 10

Special Agent Briggs hung up the phone. He wasn't used to this. He lived in a world of secrecy. That part he understood. He even got the part about the different agencies not wanting to share. It sucked, but massive egos were the norm in federal agencies comprised of three letters. No one wanted to share information that might end up with someone from another three-letter agency getting the credit. It was sad, even childish, but it was the human condition.

But this was different somehow. Discovering the crash site of *The Wonder Boys* was the top headline all over the world. Briggs was the person who found it—at least, as far as the agencies were concerned. He should have been given the heads-up if there was something unusual about it. He wasn't looking for praise or even attention. He was happy staying in the shadows. But what he did want was respect. Shutting him out—shutting out the FBI altogether—was disrespectful at the highest levels.

There was a reason for it, and he was going to figure it out. Usually, he couldn't care less about the politics of it all. In fact, one of the reasons he chose the Alaska assignment was to get as far away from the politics as possible. But somehow, this was personal. He felt a connection to the discovery and to Scott and

Michaela.

The CIA was covering it up for a reason. But why? Briggs had some vacation days, and now that he wasn't needed for anything related to the crash, he may as well use them to do some of his own investigating. He would just have to be extra careful not to leave any cyber fingerprints. The minute the CIA found out he was investigating on his own, there would be hell to pay.

He had a feeling his boss suspected that the vacation wasn't just a vacation. His last words as Briggs left for the day were, "Behave yourself. Don't do anything stupid."

Were his plans stupid? Probably. But he had never gotten anything accomplished by sitting back and doing nothing.

So, his first day on vacation was spent in a Starbucks, making notes the old-fashioned, non-traceable way—in a real live notebook, not online. What could the CIA be focusing on? It had to be the seventh passenger. Only six passengers were officially on the flight—the three band members and three roadies. Briggs wondered if there was any record of the roadies' names. There had to be. In fact, it was pretty simple to find the list. The media covering the story had listed everyone on the plane. He opened his newspaper—another part of his attempt to leave no cyber footprints by not going online—and immediately found the list. Besides the pilots and the band, there were three roadies: Paul Van Pelt, Adam Hardy, and Steve Brown. So, who was the extra person?

But then there was the other question: what happened to the band's manager, Chat Olson? How was he related to all this? He disappeared, never to be found. Was he killed? Was he part of whatever this conspiracy was? There were records of him staying in a hotel in Seattle the night his band disappeared. But he checked out the next morning and was never seen again.

Well, he knew where he could start. He left the Starbucks and walked to a park. It had warmed up some, so the walk felt good. He pulled a burner phone from his pocket and pressed speed dial. It called another burner phone.

The person picked up immediately.

"I shouldn't be talking to you," said the voice. "You know that, right?"

"But you will anyway because I'm irresistible."

"That wouldn't work for me if I were a woman, and it definitely won't work for me as a guy. I wouldn't use the word irresistible to describe you. 'Pain in the butt' is more accurate."

Marty Young and Briggs went to FBI school together. They were roommates and best friends. After a few years working in the FBI forensics lab and making a name for himself, Marty was offered the same job with the CIA at almost twice the pay. It worked well for Briggs and Young, as they kept the back channels open and passed on information that the other couldn't get otherwise.

"Seriously," said Marty, "they know we're friends. I don't think they know that we share information, but the fact that we are friends resulted in a special memo to me not to share any information about a certain case with anyone. I assume that's why you are calling."

"Marty, I just need to know a couple of things. I was there from the beginning, and I don't appreciate being pushed out."

"I get it, and I'll help where possible, but try to make your requests simple. Requests that don't require a lot of explanation."

"Can you talk?" asked Briggs.

"At the moment, I can. I'm on a busy city street on my way to lunch."

"What can you tell me about there being seven passengers

instead of six?"

"The person who wasn't supposed to be on the plane was Linus Cutter, a CIA agent. I can't tell you any more about him than that. It's all classified. Well beyond my pay grade."

"So he was the seventh passenger," said Briggs.

"Depends on how you look at it."

"What do you mean?"

"That license you found, the one for Travis Miller?"

"I wasn't the one who found it, but what about it?"

"Travis Miller doesn't exist," said Marty.

"In what way doesn't he exist?" asked Briggs. "Are you saying that the license doesn't go with the bones it was found in?"

"No," said Marty. "Understand, it's still early in the forensic process, but I can already tell you that those bones are not those of someone named Travis Miller. Other than the driver's license, there was no Travis Miller. There are no records of him anywhere. There is no DNA match at all to the bones. We looked at dental records. Again, a bust. What I can tell you is that he wasn't American. The dental work looked European—probably Eastern European."

"Russian?"

"Maybe."

"Then Travis Miller probably wasn't his real name."

"I can almost guarantee that it wasn't. Whatever the case, Travis Miller didn't exist. But I can't tell you more than that because I honestly don't know anything else. Oh, and one of the roadies who was supposed to be on that flight, Steve Brown, wasn't. None of the remains belonged to him."

"So, two of the roadies," Briggs looked at his list, "Van Pelt and Hardy were on the flight, but not Brown?"

"Exactly."

Briggs heard Marty ordering a hot dog from a vendor; then he came back on the line.

"Those will kill you," said Briggs.

"Then I'll go out happy."

Marty took a bite. Briggs waited for him to swallow, and then Marty said, "Look, all I can tell you is that there were two people who shouldn't have been on that flight."

"So the seventh passenger …" started Briggs.

"Could be either one of them," said Marty.

He took another bite, then swallowed.

"Take your pick. CIA agent Linus Cutter, or the nonexistent Travis Miller. If you're looking to solve a mystery, I'd guess it begins with those two."

Chapter 11

ANCHORAGE, ALASKA — 1966

Travis Miller. That was the name the man went by. A nice, innocuous American-sounding name. But Linus Cutter knew that he was as Russian as they came.

It had taken Linus many weeks to root out Travis Miller, and it wasn't easy. His CIA coworkers thought he was chasing air. There were times when he wasn't sure they were wrong. His bosses were ready to transfer him to another case. The rumors were that Miller—or whatever his name was—worked for a major arms dealer. A Russian arms dealer. The rumor was also that Miller was heading to Alaska to make a big buy. Linus's superiors were worried about something, but so far, the information hadn't made it down to Linus's level. Arms deals were always big, but this was something different. To scare them like that meant that this was really big. But was it? These days, his superiors were worried about a lot of things.

Everyone called it the Cold War. But to Linus, there was nothing cold about it. The fears of the American people—and probably also the Soviet people—were real. Schools regularly had air-raid practices. The kids were told to hide under their desks. Or they were herded into the hallway and told to lean against the wall and cover their heads. Did anyone really think it would protect them against a nuclear attack? If it weren't so scary for the public, it would be funny.

But there was nothing funny about the war Linus was involved in. His team was responsible for tracking down Soviet agents—or, in this case, Soviet arms dealers. The threat was very real. These people could wreak havoc and do irreparable damage to the United States.

And now, they were dealing with the rumor of the Soviet arms deal going down on U.S. soil. That was a scary thought. If true, were they planning to use the weapons in the U.S.?

Not everyone was convinced that the rumor was real. Even some of his fellow agents didn't believe it. But someone had to chase it down. His bosses had assigned it to Linus.

The problem was figuring out the where, the when, and the who. It meant that Linus had nothing at all—just a rumor. But it was a rumor from three different sources, all reliable. But they, too, had no more information than that. So, after a month, he was no closer to finding anything tangible than he was on the first day.

And then he caught a break. A friend in the FBI told him about a phone call overheard the day before in a sleazy hotel in Anchorage, Alaska. The caller was using a pay phone in the hotel's lobby and was speaking Russian. Unbeknownst to the caller, the hotel manager spoke some Russian, having had Russian grandparents.

When Linus questioned the coincidence, his friend reminded him that Alaska once belonged to Russia.

"It's not uncommon to find someone up there who speaks some Russian," he said.

The hotel manager couldn't hear it all, but he heard him use the word "munitions" and felt that he was taking orders from someone. Something about the call didn't feel right to him. When the caller returned to his room, the manager called a friend on the police force. His friend called a friend in the FBI, who told Linus's friend about it, making its way to Linus in record time.

"What's the man's name?" asked Linus.

His friend shuffled some papers on the other end, then said, "Travis Miller."

"I'm on my way," said Linus. "I'm leaving now."

Late that night, after an excruciatingly long flight, Linus checked into the hotel, across the hall from Travis Miller.

That was two days ago, and Linus wasn't any closer to finding out who Travis Miller was or what he was doing in Anchorage. And no one had any information on the man. Nothing but a name. It was like he didn't exist.

Well, he existed all right. Linus could attest to that.

The next day, *The Wonder Boys* came to town, and Miller suddenly worked onstage as a roadie, testing microphones, moving speakers, carrying drums and guitars, and doing everything else a roadie does. That didn't make any sense to Linus.

Through some discreet investigating, Linus learned that one of their regular roadies disappeared when they arrived in Anchorage. It just happened to be at the same time Travis Miller showed up on the scene. He seemed to know what his duties would be, so their manager, Chat Olson, hired him on the spot.

And then this morning, Miller checked out of the hotel and caught a cab to Anchorage International Airport, bags in hand. Linus heard that the band was flying to Fairbanks, where Miller must've been heading. Linus had to get on that plane.

Using his CIA badge, Linus convinced the airport officials

to summon the band's manager, Chat Olson, to a meeting. Once there, Linus explained that he had to get to Fairbanks quietly and asked if he could hitch a ride with them. Chat agreed, promising to keep quiet about Linus's profession.

But Linus didn't just want a ride. He wanted a ride in the same plane as Travis Miller. He needed to keep an eye on him.

Linus was taken down to the plane and escorted onboard. He introduced himself to everyone, including Travis Miller. His story was that he worked for the FAA undercover and had to get to Fairbanks without anyone knowing he was coming. His presence on the plane was secret—he didn't exist in their eyes.

On that snowy night in Anchorage, CIA agent Linus Cutter would never be heard from again.

Chapter 12

PRESENT DAY

"Who were they?"

Derek Prescott sat in his Long Island mansion, talking on a phone that had been swept so many times for bugs that he felt he should be in the extermination business.

And in many ways, he was. One of the top arms dealers in the world, Prescott had managed to remain mostly under the radar. Derek Prescott wasn't his real name. Seen as a successful importer and philanthropist, no one knew his real profession. As an arms dealer, he was a ghost. In fact, his nickname was The Ghost. All the Feds knew about The Ghost was that he was the son of the man known only as The Russian. The Russian disappeared many years earlier, but his son, only a teenager at the time, took over his father's business immediately upon his disappearance. He quickly developed a reputation as a ruthless businessman—maybe even more ruthless than his father. The Feds didn't know who The Ghost was, just as they had never learned the real identity of The Russian. But what they did know was that thousands of innocent people had died from the arms that he—and his father before him—peddled.

"Just a couple of guys," said the woman.

"'Just a couple of guys' doesn't cut it. What did you do with them?"

"We let them go."

"You what?"

"We let them go. They have no idea what we're doing, and it seemed wiser to let them go than to kill them and risk an investigation. One of the men had been here before. There was a plane crash a few miles away. He had come to investigate it."

"That was near you?"

"A couple of miles away."

"A second ago, you said it was a few miles away."

"What's the big deal?" asked the woman.

"It's only one of the most talked-about news stories in the world. Watch out for planes and helicopters. You don't want to be seen."

"We've seen a few in the distance, but nothing close to us."

"Yeah, well, keep your eye out."

Prescott did not doubt that she would. Gwen Slade was her name. A former ATF agent, Prescott had found her a few years before when one of his men made a fatal mistake and tried to sell some arms to Slade, who was working undercover. Slade was smart and managed to find the connection between the man and Prescott. She was the only person who had ever done that.

The man's mistake was fatal only because Prescott had him killed before he could be arraigned.

As for Slade, everyone has a price, and Prescott made her an offer she couldn't refuse. For her, the difference between enforcing the law and breaking it was tenuous. She quickly became one of his his most valued employees, and he could trust her with the most delicate assignments.

Prescott didn't tell Slade that he was one of the few people in the world who knew that there was a connection between that flight and the mission he had sent the woman and her team on. She didn't need to know.

He knew that a man named Travis Miller had been on that plane to meet with some people who had stolen a very important shipment of weapons. Prescott knew what the weapons were and why his father was so anxious to obtain them. He also knew that his father lost a lot of money on the deal, and how it happened. His father explained all that to him. But what he hadn't told him was where the weapons were stored. He knew it was up in Alaska someplace. But Alaska was one big-ass state! It could be anywhere.

He had recently put out feelers to people retired from the covert agencies—in particular, the KGB. None of the agents from that time would still be alive, but maybe the story had been passed down. Chances were slim that the inquiries would pan out, but it was always possible.

But luck had finally turned in his favor. Someone remembered something, and for a large sum of money, he could tell Prescott where the meeting from sixty years earlier took place. That was all the information he had, but it was something.

Prescott sent Slade and her team out there. They found the site of the meeting but no evidence of any weapons.

But Prescott knew that the weapons had been there, and also knew that they had never surfaced for sale at any time in the last sixty years. Prescott had his finger on the pulse of the arms market. He would have known.

But where were they?

His father picked and chose which deals he wanted his son involved in. It was also one of the reasons Prescott had hated him. His father said that it was part of the training process. To an ambitious teenager, it was simply a form of control.

"How do you know the men won't talk?" he asked Slade.

"The first time one of the guys showed up..."

"The first time?" Prescott interrupted.

"He's been here three times." Prescott sensed a sudden nervousness in her voice, which was unusual for her. "The first time he came, he was with a young girl. So, when he showed up the last time, we threatened to harm her if he told anyone."

"Can you follow up on that threat?"

"We could if we needed to. We have his name and address. He's a bush pilot from Homer, Alaska. But to send someone over to Homer would leave us short-handed."

"You said he came by three times," Prescott said.

"The second time, he brought a bunch of Feds—FBI and NTSB. They must have been going to the crash site. He returned to his plane with a few of them, and they left, but we haven't seen them since then."

"I read that they created space near the crash site for the investigative team," said Prescott. "You probably won't see them again, but this pilot worries me. If he shows up again, you take action. Got it?"

"Got it."

"So?" he asked.

"So what?" she answered.

"Have you made any headway?"

"Not yet, but we will."

"Famous last words."

"Have I ever failed you?"

"There's always a first time."

"We've searched everywhere around here," Slade said, annoyed at her boss's comment.

"And?"

"Nothing yet."

"It has to be there."

"And if it's here, we'll find it. We think it's probably nearby—underground maybe—but we're still looking."

"You better find it soon because you have another problem."

"What's that?" asked the woman.

"Word is, someone else has obtained some of the same information we have. You might have some company—and not the friendly type."

"Who is it?"

"Russian versions of you."

"I thought you were the Russian version of us."

"Funny. These are freelance KGB contractors."

"Shit," said Slade. "If the KGB knows, it's only a matter of time before others get the same information. Mossad, MI-6, CIA. It's going to be crowded up here."

"Which is why the clock is ticking."

"Are you absolutely sure it's here?" asked Slade.

"Positive."

"Then we'll keep looking."

Prescott hung up, frowning. They had to find it. He'd make a fortune—more of a fortune than he already had.

But, if Slade and her team did find it, they better be extra careful.

One screw-up could be devastating.

Chapter 13

"I shouldn't be telling you this, Scott," said Briggs.

He had called me on a number I didn't recognize.

"You said that a couple of days ago," I said.

"I meant it then, and I mean it now. There's some heavy-duty shit going down here. I found out a little—no need for you to know how I found out—but it's not much. The person who told me was taking a chance."

"Is that why you've called me on an unfamiliar number?"

"It's a burner phone."

"Should I be worried?"

"About your phone? No. In my case, my official phone is government-issued, so they can track all kinds of stuff on it. That's why I'm using this phone. You don't have to worry."

"Okay."

"By the way, I'm on vacation for a few days. I wanted a little time to research some of this without anyone looking over my shoulder. If you need to call me, call this phone. Here's what I know. You had the band, the two pilots, and two roadies. So, that's five passengers plus the pilots. Then you had a CIA agent named Linus Cutter. I don't know his story. I don't know why he was there. Travis Miller is the last one. As far as I can tell, no one knows who he is—or was—including the CIA.

Travis Miller doesn't exist. Based on his dental work, they think he may have been Russian, but that's as much as they know. Or, I should say, it's as much as my source knows. Does someone know who he is? Maybe. I don't know if they've done, or are planning to do, any ancestry testing. It's all a big secret. So, you have to be extra careful. You should leave all this stuff alone."

*****

Although Briggs's information was interesting, it didn't help the situation, so I had to move on.

Anyone who knows me could tell you that I have a problem. When I get something in my head, it's hard to get rid of it. Maybe that's why Max and I get along so well—I'm like a dog with a bone.

I also hate it when someone has wronged me or, especially, someone I love. When they shot at Jon and me, they wronged us. But when they brought up Michaela, that put it on a completely different level. They actually had the nerve to threaten a child?

So, I got it into my head to retaliate. I decided to head back up there and look over the situation. They were there for a reason. I just had to figure out what it was. Maybe Briggs was right. Maybe they were poachers. If so, they needed to be dealt with.

Poaching had been a problem in Alaska for a long time, with trophy hunters going after grizzlies, other bears, elk, moose, and countless other animals.

If they were poachers, maybe if I buzzed the area a little, it would scare the animals away—or even scare the poachers away.

Was I considering all this just to annoy or disrupt them? Maybe. But the fact that they stole my registration told me they were worried. And if they were worried about me, maybe I should be worried about them.

Max had been on a lot of my trips lately, so I felt he needed some time at home. He could play outside with Slob, my other dog, a monster of an animal who kept to himself and showed up whenever he felt like it. Max had an image to keep up in public and showed nothing but disdain toward Slob, but in private, they loved playing together.

So, the day after Jon and I had our encounter with the woman and her friends, I was back in the air and on my way to visit them again. This time, however, I'd stay in the air. And I'd do this on my own. There was no sense in involving Jon.

Somehow, the poacher theory didn't feel right to me. There was something more quasi-military about this group. I had seen a few poachers in my years in Alaska, and these people didn't fit the bill.

It was a beautiful fall day—cold but sunny. Hopefully, the bright sun would make it easier to see anything they might be doing down there. I also wanted to look for another landing strip. They had to get there somehow; another landing spot was the only thing that made sense.

Was I putting Michaela in danger by my actions? I didn't think so. Briggs was probably right about that. Would they really have someone sitting around in Homer waiting for word to harm Michaela? Of course not. It didn't make sense. They were just trying to scare me. Well, it had the opposite effect.

As I approached the area, I saw a couple of helicopters in the distance—probably news choppers over the crash site. I'd heard that the NTSB had removed all the debris and was in cleanup mode. By tomorrow, the crash site would be empty.

I was glad the authorities had managed to keep my name out of the news. I was just known as "a bush pilot" who spotted the wreckage.

I flew over the valley where I had made three previous landings. All seemed quiet. I remained at an altitude out of rifle range, just in case. I would make a lower pass a bit later. For now, I wanted to get a general idea of what I was dealing with and to see if there was another landing strip in the area.

A minute later, I saw it. I was coming up on another narrow valley. It looked long enough to land a small plane. I didn't see anything at first. And then I did. Covered in branches and brush at the end of the valley was a plane. They had done a decent job of hiding it. Anyone not looking for it would have missed it. However, I was looking for it.

I had an idea, but it would mean dropping to just a couple hundred feet above the valley. Maybe from that altitude, the tail numbers would be visible. It was worth a try.

I made a wide turn, descending rapidly. I suddenly had a flashback to my crash in the forest a few months earlier. Not a fun memory.

I sailed over the forest at an altitude well within rifle range. But nothing clanged against the fuselage or shot through the windshield.

I reached the valley and immediately saw the tail number on the plane. I quickly memorized it, then climbed to a much more comfortable altitude, where I quickly wrote down the numbers. Just because I memorized them now didn't mean I would remember them an hour from now.

When I returned home, I would run the numbers through the FAA Registry Database.

In the meantime, I wanted to see if anything popped out at

me on the ground. It wouldn't be easy since it was a heavily forested area, but it was worth a try. The dense foliage might help me avoid getting shot at, too. It's hard to get a clear shot through the trees, especially when shooting at a target speeding by.

I again descended to an altitude of about a thousand feet. It would be close enough to see something out of place but not too close to the tops of the trees. I started looking when I reached my valley, and when I reached the second valley, I turned to begin the process again.

I made two passes and saw nothing of interest. I decided to give it one more try.

The third time was a charm. I saw something!

I made another turn and came back over the spot.

Tents! They were camouflaged, but I could see parts of them. But there was something else. They were much closer to the second valley than the one I had landed in.

I would need another fly-by to get another look at it.

So, once again, I came around, this time ignoring the tents and concentrating on whatever the other thing was.

It looked like part of a building.

A building? Out here?

Did I dare one more fly by? My gut told me no, but my gut and brain weren't always on the same page.

I dropped down a couple hundred feet for a closer look and passed over it. I couldn't see much, but the building wasn't large—maybe a cabin? But, like the plane crash, it looked old and overgrown.

That was as much as I was going to see. It was time to go home.

Then I heard a sharp clanging noise. And again. There it was. Now they were shooting at me. Only two rounds hit the plane. I would have to hope they didn't hit anything vital.

I climbed to about 8,000 feet and started on my way home, glancing constantly at my instrument panel. After about ten minutes, I assured myself that the airplane was okay. Now, I felt calm enough to think about what I saw.

What *did* I see?

Their tents were less than a mile from the second valley but at least two or three miles from where we encountered the group. If they had gone all the way to the first valley, it made me think they were looking for something. But what? The poacher theory still wasn't out of the question.

But what was the building?

And did it play a role in all this?

Chapter 14

As soon as I returned to Homer, I checked out my plane. I found the two spots that were hit. Both rounds had hit the plane at an angle, leaving a scar but not a hole.

When I got home, I checked out the tail numbers on the FAA Registry Database. The plane was registered to a company based in the Cayman Islands. I could tell immediately that it was a shell company. I'd never find any information on them. If I felt it was necessary, I'd look into it further down the line.

I spent the rest of the day deciding whether or not to tell Michaela about the group in the woods. I didn't want to, but at the same time, they had made threats, and it would be important for Michaela to keep her eyes open just in case.

"How was your day?" I asked when I picked her up from school. She had stayed late to work on a project and called me a few minutes earlier to say she was ready. She was standing outside the school with another girl whose parents had just arrived.

"Good. Making headway on the project," she said, getting in the truck.

I had forgotten what the project was and didn't want to look stupid, so I just said, "Good." I figured she'd give me a clue later. Sadly, Michaela was smarter than me.

"I bet you don't remember what the project is," she said.

"Um."

"A history of the Yukon Gold Rush."

"Oh yeah, right."

"Ha. I never told you what it was. I just wanted to see you squirm."

"I swear I'm going to drop you from the plane the next time we're up there. Who's your friend?"

"Sally," said Michaela. "She's pretty cool and really smart. We kinda connected, and now we're working on the project together."

I was happy to hear that. Michaela needed some friends her age.

As we were driving home, I said, "I have a job for you."

"Wait. Another?"

"What do you mean?"

"You already passed off one job on me—to research *The Wonder Boys* and their fateful trip. Do you actually do anything?"

"I delegate."

She gave me a sour look.

"Besides, I've changed my mind. I'm going to research the history of it myself. I need to get up to speed on it."

"You need to get up to speed on a lot of things," said Michaela. "Mostly dinner. I'm starving."

I suddenly realized that I was, too.

"I'm going to have to teach you how to cook," I said.

"Another chore to delegate?"

"Hey, you go with your strengths."

We both chuckled.

"This is actually serious," I said.

"What do you mean?"

"I've been busy."

I told her about going up with Jon and getting shot at the day before. Her mouth dropped open.

"You could have been killed. Don't do that again—unless you take me with you. You need more firepower."

"You've become bloodthirsty."

"I have to protect you," she said.

"Yeah, well, I went up there again today."

"Scott, stop it! Are you trying to make me an orphan again?"

"I'm sorry, but I had to figure out what they were doing. I stayed in the air this time."

"And I bet they shot at you."

"Well … yes, but only at the end. Only two bullets hit the plane, and nothing was damaged. I promise not to do anything stupid again."

"Yeah, right."

"I saw their camp, but I saw something else, too—part of a small building."

"Which you are not going to check out, right?"

"Right. But that's not why I brought all this up. Your job is to be watchful."

"What do you mean?"

I described our encounter with the woman and her group and her threat toward Michaela.

"I talked to Agent Briggs," I said.

"*Special* Agent Briggs," corrected Michaela.

"Whatever. Anyway, he assured me that there was no reason for them to do anything to you and that they probably didn't have the manpower to send someone down to do it. That said, I want you to be careful. Keep your radar on. Watch what's going on around you."

"I will. Meanwhile, you're not taking any more trips up north, right?"

"Right."

She sighed.

"You know, you're really not mature enough to have a kid."

"Tell me about it."

PART TWO

1966

Chapter 15

Travis Miller was about to tell his employer the very thing he didn't want to hear.

It wasn't supposed to happen this way. It was supposed to be easy. But somehow, these things never were.

But this one was a particular mess—a royal screw-up. It wasn't his mess, but he was the one who had to clean it up.

He was on the phone in the hotel's lobby, waiting for the call to go through to The Russian. He found that funny since he was Russian, too. But he didn't have a mysterious name like "The Russian." He had to take on a stupid American-sounding name that lacked any creativity.

"What?"

That was how The Russian always answered his phone. If he thought he was being intimidating, he was right. Travis had never met him but knew the man's violent reputation.

"This is Travis Miller," he said in Russian. "The drop wasn't made, and now I can't recover the package."

"I don't want to hear that. That package is everything."

"I know, but I can't get close enough," said Travis. "My contact was being pursued and was desperate. He put it in a difficult place."

The "package" was a briefcase containing a million dollars. The drop was to happen in Seattle. The operative delivering it to Travis was minutes away from being caught by government agents, so he hid it in the first available spot—the bottom of a large box of equipment used by *The Wonder Boys* on their tour. The man just happened to be passing the venue where *The Wonder Boys* had finished a concert. Equipment was being loaded onto a truck, and a large box hadn't been closed yet. It was an opportunity that presented itself. It wasn't a good opportunity, but it was the best he had, so the man had to take it.

When the drop was missed, Travis returned to his hotel and waited for a signal from the other operative. An hour later, the call with the explanation came.

Travis tried not to get angry about the situation. These things happened. But it meant that he now had to follow *The Wonder Boys* to their next destination—and hope that the briefcase wasn't found before he arrived.

Travis immediately found a newspaper, read about *The Wonder Boys'* tour, and saw that Anchorage was the next stop.

Anchorage? Do they even have any people up there?

From the article, it looked like they were planning a day of rest, then flying out the following day. It wasn't much time to plan his next move. He had to think fast. Luckily, thinking fast was one of his strengths.

Travis took the next flight out and was already in Anchorage when it was time to tell The Russian the story of what happened.

"Do you have a plan?" asked The Russian, after processing all that Travis had told him.

"They are headed for Anchorage next and leave tomorrow. I'm sure their plane is packed. I'm already in Anchorage, preparing for their arrival.

"And?"

"And I've researched them from a fan magazine in the airport. They have three workers—they call them roadies. If one suddenly disappears, they will need another. When they arrive, I will follow one of them and make sure he is gone for good. Then I'll apply to their manager. I can be very convincing."

"And if you can't recover the package?"

"I will let you know."

"We need an alternate plan in case you have a problem. We absolutely need to keep them in Alaska. I have an idea. I will talk to Dickson and have him set up a concert in Fairbanks. That should give you enough time to retrieve it."

"And if I can't?"

"I'll replace their pilots with two of our own. From Fairbanks, we will fly them to the site; you can deal with them there. You will need to go there anyway to deliver the package. You will also take care of some loose ends."

"The munitions people?"

"Yes. Inspect the site. Make sure everything is there that I was promised. Pay the contact, send him to the plane, and then kill anyone who is left. The plane will take him to a prearranged site in Canada, where he will be paid the other half of his money. The pilots will return the next day and take you back to Anchorage. You can find your way home from there. This way, the seller gets his money—which is all he cares about—and none of the seller's people will be left at the site. We'll move our people in, and I will start the bidding process."

"Understood."

Travis hung up, not noticing the desk clerk dialing his phone.

*****

Everything worked as planned. Well, almost everything. As soon as the plane carrying *The Wonder Boys* landed, Travis lured one of the roadies away with the promise of extra cash if he would help Travis with something. Travis made sure his body would never be found.

He waited a few hours before approaching the band's manager, Chat Olson. The manager was stuck and hired Travis on the spot.

The problem was that the large crate the operative used to hide the package was the sole domain of one of the other roadies. He made it clear that no one but him ever touched the crate's contents. The man hovered over the crate like a mother hen protecting her young. Luckily, the roadie hadn't yet discovered the briefcase. Travis wasn't sure he would, as the operative said he had hidden it under some old drop cloths at the bottom of the crate.

When Travis reported it to The Russian—this time from a phone booth—the man was understandably frustrated.

"No possible way?"

"Not without killing the man, which would create a whole new set of problems."

"Okay. Dickson has arranged a concert in Fairbanks."

"Yes, Olson announced it to the band a little while ago."

"I've been thinking," said The Russian. "If you can't get it now, you might not be able to get it in Fairbanks either, so there is only one solution. Forget Fairbanks. I'll make sure the pilots take the plane directly to the site."

"And the band?" asked Travis, already knowing the

answer.

"Collateral damage."

Whoa, thought Travis. *That will create news.*

"I will be in Anchorage to meet with Dickson," continued The Russian. "If I have any further instructions, I will contact you."

"How will I know you?"

This was Travis's first job for The Russian.

"You don't need to. I know you. You just worry about getting the plane to the site and completing the deal."

The Russian hung up.

Travis, still holding the receiver, blew some air through his teeth.

It was getting interesting.

Chapter 16

Travis had never been to the meeting site but had heard about it. Or rather, he had heard the rumors about it.

Very few people knew its location—and by very few, he knew that it wasn't more than a handful. According to the rumors, it was built in the late 1950s. It consisted of a series of tunnels built by prisoners from Siberia. He never heard what happened to the prisoners afterward, but he could guess. The same thing probably happened to the project managers and architects involved in its construction.

Travis wasn't sure how many members of the Soviet government knew about it, but he assumed not very many. They only needed one high-level official to be able to transfer the prisoners from Siberia. From what he heard, a fringe group was responsible for its existence.

The purpose of the "bunker"—the only name he had ever heard it called—was as a first-strike location should the Soviet Union decide to invade America. Again, it was all rumor, but he had heard of a similar bunker in Mexico near the U.S. border, and one in North Dakota. Travis thought that it was pretty ballsy of them to build a bunker right under the Americans' noses. The bunkers were to be used as storage locations for munitions—enough munitions to supply hundreds of men, whose purpose was to break into smaller groups and secretly invade small cities. Taking out the smaller cities would send America into panic mode, making a large-scale invasion easier.

Did Travis think it could work? No. Of course not. He had to remember that it was the work of a fringe group. Fringe groups were rarely successful in these types of plans.

Evidently, the leaders of the group must have come to the same conclusion, because they had contacted The Russian to sell him their arms. The Russian couldn't care less about most of what was down there. But there was one very special batch of items that interested him. And that was what Travis was paying for. Travis would inspect them, and if they were as good as advertised, The Russian would happily let Travis hand over the money.

Could they double-cross him? There was no way that would happen. The one thing nobody wanted was to get on the wrong side of The Russian!

The Russian. Was it a mistake for Travis to take a job with him? After all, he'd had a solid career working as a KGB operative. It was his reputation that had put him on The Russian's radar. He always got the job done quietly and efficiently.

So, when The Russian offered him a job at four times the salary he was earning with the KGB, he accepted. His KGB handlers weren't happy, but there wasn't much they could do about it. Even they didn't want to get on the bad side of The Russian. After all, they used his services regularly.

The Russian was generous to those employees he valued but was vicious to those who disappointed or betrayed him. That made it even more imperative that Travis succeed in this mission. There was a lot of money at stake. The million dollars he was charged with delivering was only half of what The Russian was paying for the munitions. Or rather, only half of what he was paying for the *special* products. Next to those, the regular munitions were practically worthless.

And then there was Dickson. The man really was a music promoter. But he was also someone The Russian had used several times before as a middleman in the arms deals. Like everyone else The Russian employed, his value was tenuous. As long as he produced, he'd be paid well. When he stopped producing, he would die.

It was rumored that The Russian had a son. He should have named him "The Russian, Jr." Travis chuckled. From what he understood, the boy was only a teenager but was already becoming just as dangerous as his father. And he also had a codename. It was The Ghost. It was said that The Russian had been grooming his son from an early age to eventually take over his business.

No one had ever met The Ghost, which was precisely how The Russian had planned it. And no one would until the time came to pass the business on to him.

This was why Travis couldn't afford to screw this up. He was in a good situation, making a lot of money and working for a business that would be secure for a long time. It was a sweet deal.

If he accomplished his mission.

*****

Everything was ready. The pilots were in place and knew their roles. Travis would wait until they landed to dispose of the passengers. The exchange would be over in a few hours, and Travis would be on his way home, waiting for his next assignment.

If he did his job, the world would never know what happened to *The Wonder Boys.*

He took his seat.

This should go smoothly, he thought.

Then a man entered the plane. He looked vaguely familiar, but he couldn't place the face. What was he doing onboard this flight? And then it hit him. He had seen the man at the hotel and several times on the street. There was only one explanation. He was following Travis.

The trip just got complicated.

Chapter 17

Linus Cutter hoped he was doing the right thing. Getting on the plane with the person he was tailing was like going into a lion's den. Did Travis Miller suspect anything?

But he had no choice. He had to know where Miller was going. Linus was pretty sure that Fairbanks wasn't Miller's final destination, but he had to follow him there. The other thing he had to know was why this plane? Why didn't he charter a smaller aircraft, where he could have made the trip anonymously?

As he entered the airplane, everyone looked at him. *The Wonder Boys* all had puzzled expressions, while Travis Miller looked suspicious.

"Hi, my name is Linus Cutter. I'm from the FAA, and your manager, Mr. Olson, has permitted me to ride with you boys to Fairbanks. I have to go incognito…"

"In what?" asked Arlo.

Linus smiled. "Incognito. It means I have to go in secret. Some issues there need taking care of, but I don't want them to know I'm coming."

"So you can catch them in the act?" asked Frankie.

"Something like that. But I won't bother y'all. Pretend I'm not here. I'm just hitching a ride. By the way, I love your music."

In truth, he hated *The Wonder Boys.* Linus was more a jazz man. But there had been so much publicity about them that he knew which names went to which faces. He buckled in and closed his eyes, hoping it would put Miller at ease and make him less suspicious.

No, don't close your eyes, he thought. *Wait until you are in the air for that. Let them get to know you.*

He opened his eyes and said, "I wish I had caught your concert, but the FAA has me working all kinds of hours. How'd it go?"

"It was kind of small," said the one Linus recognized as Holt. "Chat told us we had to do one in Alaska to show that we are all about sharing our music rather than just being in it for the money."

"But we *are* in it for the money," said Arlo, laughing.

"We had a lot of military personnel from Elmendorf," said one of the roadies.

He sounds more intelligent than the band members, thought Linus. *He used the term 'personnel.' I'll bet the band doesn't even know that word.*

"It's good to have a concert for the military," said Linus. "Especially with the war going on."

"We shouldn't be there," said the roadie.

"Yeah, we should," said Frankie. "Gotta wipe out those gooks."

"Then why aren't you there?" asked the roadie.

Linus had a feeling this was not an isolated conversation.

Frankie went quiet. Linus knew why. Someone must have paid a lot of money to exempt the band from the draft.

"Why aren't you?" asked Frankie, glaring at the roadie.

"I'm 4-F due to my knees. I'd go if I could, even though I

think it's wrong."

Linus doubted it. That was an easy thing to say if you knew you couldn't go. It was time to change the subject.

"Fairbanks isn't huge," he said. "Is it worth doing a concert there?"

"I don't know," said Holt. "Chat arranged it at the last minute—some kind of favor for someone."

"Pain in the ass," said the other "real" roadie. "We should be doing large concerts. Coming up here to Eskimo land ain't worth it."

"Why are you complaining?" asked Holt. "You get paid the same either way."

"Cuz it's fucking cold!"

Linus laughed. "Yeah, it is."

"Have you been to Fairbanks a lot?" asked Travis.

Linus knew that the man was feeling him out. Honesty would be the best policy.

"Nope. Never. I'm not even stationed in Alaska. I work out of Chicago. They wanted me up here because no one knows me."

"What's so important that you can't tell the people in Fairbanks that you're coming?" continued Travis with his questions.

"I'm afraid I can't tell you that. Let's just say that I have to fix a situation."

The engines roared to life, making further conversation difficult. Linus buckled his seatbelt and prepared for takeoff.

He thought about *The Wonder Boys*. For the most part, a bunch of backward hicks. The only ones who seemed even halfway intelligent were Holt Pearson, who was the band's songwriter, and that first roadie who spoke. The rest of them seemed like total idiots.

Except, of course, Travis Miller. Linus could already tell that the man was cold and calculating. This wasn't going to be easy.

But he was in deep now. There was no turning back.

Chapter 18

The plane took off in the snow and the wind and slowly climbed to cruising altitude. The wind made the take-off a little bumpy, silencing *The Wonder Boys*, who all looked nervous. Linus opened his eyes to find Miller staring at him.

"Can I help you?" asked Linus.

"Nope."

But he kept staring.

Linus opened his briefcase and pretended to go through some papers. In actuality, the papers in the briefcase were blank, as were the folders they were in. It was a last-minute decision. If he was really from the FAA, he had to look the part. Carrying a briefcase with papers seemed the best option. He had quickly bought the briefcase from a shop in the airport and had gotten the blank paper and file folders from a secretary in the airport manager's office.

The plane took off going north, toward Fairbanks, but ten minutes into the flight, Linus felt it descending. That was curious. Were they landing? The aircraft seemed to come down to a low altitude before leveling off.

Suddenly, Linus knew why. They wanted to avoid radar. That didn't bode well. Linus knew that the massive earthquake that hit Alaska in 1964 had caused a lot of damage to the airport—damage that was still being dealt with two years later. As such, the radar had been spotty. He figured that the plane probably wasn't being tracked anyway, due to the equipment issues, but this was added insurance on their part. They had another plan in mind if they were trying to avoid radar.

He felt the plane turn to the left.

Now, he was on high alert. By turning left, they were now going west, which wasn't anywhere near Fairbanks. He was supposed to be with the FAA, so he should notice the change in direction. He decided to ignore the plane's altitude.

"Are we going west now?" he asked no one in particular. He had to speak up from the noise of the engine.

"Beats me," said Arlo.

Travis Miller didn't say a word. He was sitting across the aisle watching Linus.

He suspects something, thought Linus. *This was a bad idea.*

"Maybe I'll ask the pilot," said Linus.

He got up out of his seat and walked to the cockpit.

"Did we just turn west?" he asked.

"We did," answered the pilot. "We have to go around a weather system. It's nothing to be worried about, though. It's also why we are flying lower, in case you noticed."

Linus knew little about planes, but that didn't make sense. Shouldn't they fly higher to go above the system? He would have to stay alert.

Linus returned to his seat, all the time feeling Travis's glare.

A few minutes later, Linus felt another change in direction, again to the left. That meant they were now heading south. Back to Anchorage? No. They were west of Anchorage now. If they were going south, they'd bypass Anchorage altogether.

There was nothing he could do about it, so Linus decided

to let things play out.

A half-hour passed, and Linus felt the plane begin to slow and descend even more. It was gradual, but they were definitely heading downward. They were going to land somewhere. It was dark, so Linus couldn't see anything outside.

"Are you really FAA?" asked Travis.

"Of course. Why wouldn't I be?"

He looked over at Travis, who had a gun pointed at him.

"Because you're following me, and I have no connection to the FAA. You were staying in my hotel, and I saw you once out on the street, tailing me."

"Whoa, I'm afraid you have me confused with someone else. Can you please put down the gun?"

"Hey, man," said Arlo. "What are you doing with a gun?"

Travis turned his head slightly at the question, and Linus jumped up. He had unlatched his seatbelt at Travis's first question.

Travis saw the movement and fired, hitting Linus in the side. Linus fell onto the floor of the plane.

Travis stood up and pointed his gun at Arlo, who was staring at him with his mouth wide open in surprise. It would have to be done now. It was earlier than he intended, but Travis had no choice.

"Sorry, guys."

Travis pulled the trigger. A red stain appeared on Arlo's chest. He took two steps back and fell to the floor.

There was chaos in the plane now. Some men stood up, and others tried to unbuckle their seatbelts.

Travis turned the gun and shot one of the roadies. He faced Frankie Dale, who was struggling with his seatbelt, and shot him in the head.

From his spot on the floor, Linus saw the co-pilot step into the cabin with a gun and start shooting. He was helping Travis. The pilots were in on it! Linus suddenly realized that he wasn't getting out of this alive.

The slaughter was quick and bloody. In seconds, *The Wonder Boys* and their roadies ceased to exist.

Travis turned back to Linus, but Linus had been able to take out his gun. He shot, spinning Travis around. Linus took a shot at the copilot but missed. The plane suddenly started diving.

His bullet had hit the pilot!

The co-pilot turned to enter the cockpit and take over the controls. Linus let him, as it was the only way he would have a chance to survive.

Across the aisle, Travis was struggling to stand up, so Linus calmly shot him again.

The plane was still descending at a rapid rate. The co-pilot had gotten into his seat, and Linus saw him struggling with the wheel. The nose of the plane was beginning to come up, but Linus saw through the cockpit windshield that they'd never make it. He could see the ground now, and they were too close.

It was all going to end here.

A moment later, the plane hit the trees.

Linus slammed into the cabin wall behind the cockpit.

He died instantly.

Chapter 19

PORTLAND, OREGON

"Marge, calm down."

Chat Olson was trying his best to get his secretary to listen to him, but she was hysterical. The phone connection was also fuzzy, further exacerbating the tense situation.

"Please calm down."

Finally, Marge stopped blubbering and caught her breath.

"I didn't know what happened to you," she said. "It's so shocking about the boys. Do you think they are dead?"

"I do," replied Chat. "Their plane must have gone down in the bad weather."

Other than the cold and a few snowflakes, the weather hadn't been bad, but he couldn't give Marge the impression that foul play was involved. He had to keep her calm because what he needed to tell her was vital.

"Where are you?" she asked.

"That doesn't matter. I need you to think straight. Has anyone come looking for me?"

"The police came by," said Marge with a sniffle. She blew her nose. "We've had lots of calls from agents and other music people, sending their prayers and thoughts about the boys."

"Anyone else?" asked Chat.

"Oh, two days ago, two men showed up at the door wanting to speak to you. They said they were from the FBI but wouldn't show me their badges. Something about them scared me."

"What did you tell them?"

"The truth. I didn't know where you were, and you hadn't contacted me. Now I can let the police know that you called."

"No, Marge. Don't do that. Listen to me carefully. Are you listening?"

"Yes," she said in a scared, high-pitched voice.

"I'm not trying to frighten you, but no one must know where I am. I can't explain it right now. You've never heard from me. Got that?"

"But…"

"No buts. When we hang up, pretend I never called. My life depends on it."

"Okay, I guess."

"You haven't heard from me since the day I called from Anchorage before the concert. Do you understand?"

"No, I don't understand, but I'll do as you ask."

"Thank you."

"When will I see you?" she asked.

"You won't. I'm dissolving my business. *The Wonder Boys* were my only clients. Just put up the CLOSED sign and walk out the door. But before you do, you know the combination to the safe, right?"

"Yes."

"In the safe is some cash—probably close to $5000. It's yours. Please take it. You've been a great employee and a good friend. I have enough cash to survive for a while, but I want you to have the money in the safe. My suggestion is that you take a vacation for a few weeks. Go to Hawaii or something."

It took Chat several attempts to convince her to take the money, but she finally relented. Remember," said Chat, "you haven't heard from me. If anyone asks why you put up the closed sign, tell them you assumed I was in the plane and disappeared with the others, and you no longer have a job."

Much to Chat's relief, Marge had calmed down and finally grasped the situation.

"Okay, Chat. It all sounds very cloak and dagger, but I trust you. I'm sorry it has ended this way. I've enjoyed working for you and being your friend. All I ask is that you take care of yourself."

"I will. You take care of yourself, too."

He hung up. Chat was happy to give Marge the money from the safe. She deserved it. And he wasn't lying about having enough cash to live on. The first thing he did after leaving the hotel was to direct the cabbie to a branch of his bank, where he took out $10,000. He had much more money in a savings account, but he didn't need it now. In fact, he had a funny feeling that he would never see that money again.

From there, Chat had the cabbie drive him to the bus station. The bus seemed to be the most anonymous way to travel, and right now, staying anonymous was important. He caught the first bus to Portland, Oregon, where he was now staying in a decent but out-of-the-way hotel. He had used a fake name when he checked in.

Chat felt that he was safely under the radar. If anyone were looking for him, he would be almost impossible to find.

He lay on the bed staring at the ceiling. What now? He couldn't run forever. Hell, he didn't even know what—or who—he was running from. The Russian, whose name he didn't know? Dickson, the promoter? He knew very little about the man.

Were they even looking for him? Maybe he was doing all this unnecessarily. Maybe they couldn't care less about him.

He suddenly missed Nancy. Their night together in the hotel was wonderful. Maybe all this would blow over, and they could get back together.

So many maybes.

He needed to hear Nancy's voice. He needed to apologize to her for leaving so suddenly and to tell her that he really did see a future with her. Damn all of them for causing him to run like this!

Chat got out of bed, put on his jacket, and left the room. He had to talk to Nancy, but not from the hotel. He'd find a phone booth and call her from there.

As he left the hotel, he looked around carefully for anyone who looked suspicious. He knew it was a needless gesture. There was no way they could have tracked him down, especially this quickly.

There was a phone booth down the block. He walked quickly to it, stepped in, and closed the door. There was something peaceful about a phone booth. It was like the peace he found in a men's room stall. Was there something wrong with him?

He put a pile of dimes on the shiny metal shelf below the phone. He didn't know how long the call would take, so he had to be ready to feed in the dimes.

Chat dialed and waited for the connection to go through.

A woman answered. She seemed upset. There was something about the way she said "Hello."

"Hi, can I speak to Nancy, please?"

Yes, she was upset. At his question, she started to cry. Uh-oh. He waited for her to calm down.

"Is there something wrong?" he asked. "Is Nancy okay?"

"Who is this?" the woman asked.

"This is Chat Olson. I'm a friend of Nancy's."

The woman let out a sob. Finally, she said, "I'm Nancy's mother."

Chat waited, dreading what he knew was coming next.

"Nancy is dead. She was murdered."

Chapter 20

The phone slipped out of Chat's hand and dangled near his knees.

Dead? Murdered? He couldn't believe it.

He grabbed the phone and brought it back to his ear. Nancy's mother was still crying.

"Can you tell me what happened?" he asked. Tears were rolling down his face.

"They—they found her in an alley behind a hotel downtown. She had been stabbed. I don't understand. Why would someone do that? She still had her purse, so they didn't rob her. They didn't do anything … anything else to her."

Chat knew what she meant. He was happy about that, at least.

"I'm—I'm so sorry," he said. "We had just connected again after many years, and I was looking forward to seeing her again."

"Yes, she told me. She called me from downtown to tell me how happy she was to see you again. It must have happened right after that phone call because she said she was coming right home. She—she never made it."

There wasn't much more that Chat could say, so he told her how sorry he was and that he would contact her for funeral information. He wouldn't, of course, because whoever killed Nancy would be watching the funeral for Chat. It would end up being his funeral.

After he hung up, he stood in the booth, not knowing what to do. He felt like he was drained of life. The tears had stopped, and he was suddenly devoid of emotion. In a span of two days, his life had been turned completely upside down.

Finally, he opened the door and walked out, leaving the stack of dimes on the shelf.

As he walked back to his hotel, emotions began to rise to the surface. It wasn't sadness or despair. It wasn't fear. It wasn't even anger. It was something else, something he had never felt in his life.

It was hatred. For the first time in his life, he wanted to kill. He wanted someone to pay—no, not just pay. He wanted someone to suffer a long and painful death. Chat had lost the boys and his business. Most of all, he had lost Nancy. In essence, he had lost everything. There was nothing more that could be taken from him.

Chat had always considered himself a man of peace. He opposed the Vietnam War. He had never owned a gun—or even shot a gun. He played by the rules. And look what it had gotten him.

Chat still believed that. He still believed that playing by the rules was the right thing to do. But he was dealing with people who didn't have the same view of life. They took what they wanted and left destruction in their path.

Well, if those were the rules they lived by, they could also be the ones they died by.

Chat got back to his hotel room and immediately took a shower. He needed to think, and he did some of his best thinking in the shower, with the hot water pounding on his head.

Twenty minutes later, he turned off the shower. He could have stayed in there much longer if the hot water hadn't run out. But it was enough. He had a plan. He'd give it a couple of weeks for things to cool down and then put it into motion.

*****

Chat let three weeks go by. He would need to go back to Seattle, and he had to make sure they weren't watching the bus station. Of course, if they were watching, they would be looking for Chat to leave Seattle, not arrive there. But chances were they'd see him if he was getting off a bus.

Three weeks seemed enough. They had to figure that he was gone by now. They probably also assumed that he was running for his life. He wasn't. He had no life left, so he had nothing to run for.

His plan was simple. Maybe it was too simple or too naïve, but it was all he could think of. He would find the promoter. Alvin Dickson was his name. Chat would force Dickson to give him the name of the Russian man. Then he'd find the Russian and kill him. Definitely naïve, but he didn't care. Maybe in the process, he would find out what it was all about. What was so important that they felt it was necessary to kill so many people?

When he got off the bus, he looked around carefully. Everything seemed fine—just the normal throng of travelers.

Chat had bought a small revolver from a sleazy pawn shop in Portland. The pawnbroker—an unhealthy older man with a cigarette always hanging out of his mouth—saw immediately that Chat knew nothing about guns. He told him that the gun was simple—you just point it and pull the trigger. Chat was happy about that. He needed simplicity.

Alvin Dickson lived in Seattle, where Chat had met him. Chat looked up his address in a phone book and then bought a city map. From the map, it looked like Dickson lived in a swanky area of town. That would make sense.

Chat checked into a small hotel near the waterfront and waited. To do what he wanted to do, he needed a cloudy, rainy day—a day when most people would be off the streets. Luckily, this was Seattle. He didn't have to wait long.

Two days later, on a cold and murky day, Chat hailed a cab and took it to a department store about a mile from Dickson's house. It would have been a long walk without the taxi, but he needed it to drop him off far enough away from Dickson's home not to draw suspicion to himself. Chat got out of the cab at the store and walked in. In case the cabbie was later asked, he needed to be seen entering the store.

He waited a few minutes, then left the store and started walking. He had a black raincoat with a large hood, which would make it difficult for anyone to identify him.

Identify him? That sounded like something from an alternate universe. Was he really doing this? Was he ready to commit a crime? Mr. Squeaky-clean? Yes, he was ready. The hatred hadn't left his thoughts. If anything, it had become more intense. These people had to be stopped. Chat had no idea what they were doing, but whatever it was had to end.

As Chat approached where Dickson lived, he recalled what he knew of the guy. It wasn't much. He knew Dickson was single, which was good. Chat didn't want to have to deal with a wife or kids. Would he have any domestic help? Chat hoped not. That might change everything.

He had already figured out how he'd do it. Chat would walk right up to the front door and knock. He wanted to see

Dickson's reaction. That would tell him a lot.

Chat was shaking. Maybe this wasn't going to be as easy as he thought. This wasn't who he was. Then again, maybe it was now. After all, he had nothing left to lose.

Chat found the house, walked up to the front door, hesitated, then knocked.

The moment of truth.

Alvin Dickson opened the door. His eyes went wide once he realized who was standing on his stoop.

Chat pulled the gun from his raincoat pocket and pointed it at Dickson.

"We need to talk."

Chapter 21

Dickson recovered quickly.

"Chat! Everyone wondered what happened to you. Why the gun? I don't understand. We're friends."

Dickson backed up, almost tripping in the process. Chat followed him and closed the door behind him.

"We're not friends," answered Chat. "We hardly know each other. You set up the concert in Anchorage, and we showed up. That's the extent of our relationship."

"Then why the gun? I thought the concert went well."

"The concert was fine. I guess I should have said that it *should* have been the extent of our relationship. But it really wasn't, was it?"

"I don't know what you mean. Are you upset with me because I asked *The Wonder Boys* to go to Fairbanks as a favor? Chat, you know that I couldn't have predicted the result. No one could. I'm sick about it."

"Uh-huh."

"I am. Of course, I am."

"Who's the Russian?"

"What Russian?"

Chat swiped the gun against the side of Dickson's head. It hit with a loud crack, and Dickson dropped to the floor, moaning.

Did he really do that? He hadn't even thought about it. It was like his arm was working autonomously from his mind.

"Why—why did you do that?" asked Dickson, holding the side of his head. Blood was seeping through his fingers.

The man looked so pitiful lying there that Chat almost questioned if he was doing the right thing.

Almost.

Then he thought back to the conversation in the bathroom.

"The Russian you were talking to in the bathroom at the Anchorage Airport."

Chat saw Dickson's face change just slightly. Then it returned to normal. He sat up.

"I don't know what you're talking about."

Chat swung the gun again. Dickson managed to get his arm up to deflect the blow from his head, but Chat heard the wrist crack. Dickson screamed in pain.

"You're a psycho!" he yelled. Then he laid back down on the floor, moaning.

"Every time you lie to me, I'm going to hit you," said Chat. "That was lie number two. I was in the bathroom in a stall when the two of you met. You didn't see me. I heard everything you said."

Dickson went silent.

Chat pointed to the living room.

"Get up and go sit on the couch. Now!"

Dickson slowly got up, using his good arm to brace himself, and moved to the couch.

"Who is he?" Chat demanded.

"Someone you don't want to mess with. He's very powerful and very dangerous."

"I'll decide who I want to mess with," said Chat. "What's his name?"

"I don't know."

Chat raised his arm, and Dickson quickly threw his good arm in the air to ward off another hit.

"Honestly, I don't know" he said quickly. "Everyone calls him 'The Russian.' If I knew his name, I'd probably be dead now."

"Understand something," said Chat. "You've ruined my life, and I have nothing to live for. You killed my band. You killed my girlfriend…"

"I had nothing to do with that," said Dickson. "That was all The Russian's doing."

"Maybe, but you knew the band was going to die."

Dickson started to say something, then stopped.

"Right?" said Chat, his voice now raised.

"You have to understand something," said Dickson. "You've stepped into something big. Really big. This is serious shit."

"Step? I didn't step into anything," said Chat. "You put me here when you killed my band and my girlfriend."

"I didn't…" He stopped when Chat raised the gun. "I'm sorry. This is too big even for me. If anyone stepped in anything, it was me. I had no idea how big this was. The Russian scares the shit out of me. I can't get out of it now. I accepted a lot of money, and I regret every dollar of it."

"Who is he, and what does he want?"

"He's an an arms dealer. All I've been able to figure is that he's making a big buy—a huge one. It's really important to him."

He looked up at Chat, blood still dripping from his head where Chat hit him.

"And he'll kill anyone who stands in his way."

Chat just shook his head. This was way beyond anything

he'd ever had to deal with.

"I didn't know," said Dickson. "I really didn't. I was tricked. All I know is that this buy is huge. Whatever is in Alaska, he won't stop until he gets it."

Chat sat on a chair across from the couch, but with his gun still pointed at Dickson. He needed to think. This was all too much. Should he go after the man called The Russian? He sounded powerful and ruthless. Should Chat go to the FBI? And tell them what? That a madman was about to buy weapons of some kind? They'd want specifics. And if he called them to Dickson's house. Dickson would tell them that Chat broke in and attacked him. Chat would find himself in jail.

Was Dickson really in over his head? He looked pretty pathetic at the moment. Blood was dripping down his face from where Chat had hit him. Was Dickson telling the truth? Was he really a pawn in all this?

And then Chat thought back to the bathroom stall. What did Dickson say?

"The pilots know where to go."

"And our man?" the Russian had asked.

"He knows, too, but the pilots will take care of the situation."

And then…

"We might have one small problem, but nothing we can't take care of quickly—Olson."

Dickson wasn't in over his head. He knew exactly what he was doing. He was in bed with The Russian.

Chat cocked the hammer. It made a scary click in the quiet room. Dickson stiffened.

"How stupid do you think I am?" asked Chat. "I heard what you said in the men's room, and it wasn't someone in over his head. You knew exactly what you were talking about. The Russian might be in charge, but you're not some unwilling patsy. You're in on it too."

Dickson was quiet for a few seconds, then something changed. In a voice dripping with malice, he said, "And what do you think you can do about it?"

"You're going to tell me where they went."

"Fat chance of that."

Chat glanced out the window. It was pouring. Good.

He calmly turned toward Dickson and pulled the trigger. At less than five feet away, even Chat couldn't miss.

The sound of the shot was deafening in the room, and Dickson's left knee exploded.

Dickson screamed. He tried to hold his knee, but it was too raw, so he hugged his thigh. Blood was soaking his pant leg. Tears ran down his face.

Chat let him cry while he considered whether anyone could have heard the shot. It was louder than he expected, but with the rain outside, he was sure no one could have heard it. Then he thought about how easy it was for him to pull the trigger. It was because he had nothing to lose.

Dickson was quietly sobbing now. He looked at Chat with fear in his eyes.

Good, thought Chat. *This is where I want him.*

"Where did the plane go?" he asked.

"I don't know."

"You are going to limp for the rest of your life. I can shoot the other one, and you'll be in a wheelchair. It's up to you."

He pulled the hammer back. He was pretty sure he didn't have to do that. The guy in the pawn shop said he just had to pull the trigger. But he liked the threatening sound it made.

"Okay, okay," said Dickson, holding up his hands. "In my top desk drawer, there's a map. It shows where they're going."

Chat moved over to the desk and put the gun down. He

wasn't worried about Dickson scrambling for it. He wouldn't be scrambling for anything ever again. Chat opened the drawer and pulled out a map right on top. It was a map of Alaska. Far south and west of Anchorage was an "X." Some numbers were next to it. Chat took them to be the latitude and longitude.

"That's where the bunker is," said Dickson. "That's what they call it—the bunker."

"And what about the plane?" asked Chat.

"I don't know," he said, grimacing. He was breathing heavily. "Christ! This hurts! The plane was supposed to land there, drop something off, then take off again. Then, they would dispose of your band. But something must have happened because our guy never made it. The plane must've crashed."

"What will I find at the bunker?"

"A whole shitload of munitions. A massive amount. It's not a place you want to go."

"And The Russian?"

"He doesn't like to get his hands dirty. But in this case, he said he might have to go there. That was a couple of weeks ago, but these things take time. So, you never know."

It was now thundering outside. It sounded more like summer than fall.

Chat picked up the gun and pointed it at Dickson.

Could I really? he thought.

A loud clap of thunder came, and Chat pulled the trigger. The round went into Dickson's chest. He was dead immediately. Chat stood there, looking at Dickson's lifeless body. He had really done that.

It was time to leave. Chat put the gun in his belt behind his back and the map in a zippered pocket of his raincoat.

And then he walked out.

Chapter 22

Chat was back in his hotel room, shaking. The magnitude of what he had just done was hitting him now. He had killed someone! He went into the bathroom and held his head over the toilet, thinking he would throw up. Surprisingly, nothing came up. He slowly stood up and left the bathroom. He was dizzy, so he lay on the bed and tried to sleep, but his mind was too active.

Okay, Dickson deserved to die for his role in what happened to *The Wonder Boys*, but should Chat have been the one to kill him? And then he thought of Nancy. Sweet Nancy. A good person with a kind heart. She didn't deserve to die.

As he thought of her, Chat knew that Dickson wouldn't be his last victim. He had to get up to Alaska, but he'd have to go soon. The snow that fell when *The Wonder Boys* were leaving didn't stick, but he figured that in another month, it would probably be snowy and impassable.

Could he find a pilot to take him up there? If he paid him enough money, he was sure he could. He might have to lie a little. On the other hand, he wouldn't want the pilot to be in any danger. But he could work that out when the time came.

The following day, Chat was at the Seattle Airport, asking small plane owners if they knew anyone who could fly him to a place southwest of Anchorage and back for a flat fee of $5000. He figured the amount would scare away the more honest folk and appeal to those willing to cross the line between legal and illegal. Not that what he wanted the plane for was illegal; he just knew that he needed someone a little tougher than the average person.

Finding someone was surprisingly easy. The man negotiated for an extra thousand and all expenses, explaining that it was a long trip—up to Juneau, over to Anchorage, then down to the spot marked on the map. Chat agreed, telling him he would give him half when they left, with the remainder to be paid at the end. They arranged to meet the next morning.

Chat had one last thing to do. He asked for some writing paper and an envelope from the hotel's front desk, then spent an hour writing a letter. He sealed it in the envelope, then headed to a branch of his bank.

That errand done, Chat ate a small meal in the hotel's restaurant. He wasn't hungry, but knew that he had to get some food into his body. Then he spent that night packing only what he'd need. He had bought a small backpack, just large enough to fit a few days' worth of clothes, toiletries, and his revolver. Is that what his life had come down to?

He didn't sleep well that night. He kept thinking about Nancy and how quickly her life was snuffed out. In some ways, it was good that he was thinking of her because it fueled the intense hatred he felt toward the late Dickson, The Russian, and anyone else involved in this.

He was up bright and early the next morning, where he caught a cab to the airport and met up with Ernie, his pilot. Chat, still using an assumed name, counted out $3000, and they were soon on their way.

Ernie wasn't much for talking, which was okay with Chat.

Besides, it was loud in the plane, making conversation difficult. Occasionally, Ernie would point something out, or Chat would ask a question, but mostly, they remained silent.

Ernie wasn't joking. It was a long trip, with stops for fuel and food. They spent the night in Juneau and again in Anchorage. Between the fuel, the food, the hotel bills, and the $6,000 commission, it was an expensive trip. But Chat didn't care. He had one mission, and he was determined to finish it. Afterward, he could call the FBI to inform them about the bunker.

And then what? What was he going to do with his life after that? He could go after The Russian, but he had a feeling he'd never find him. He couldn't go back to managing bands. No, he was done with that. Frankly, he had no idea what he would do.

"Does this place have a runway?" Ernie asked Chat the morning they were leaving Anchorage.

"I don't know. It has to. Other planes go there. I've never been there myself."

"I never asked you what's there, 'cuz I figured it was your business. But what's there?"

Chat thought that Ernie looked the part of a bush pilot. He was about sixty and skinny, with deep lines in his sunburned face. But he had an air of competence, and though he was skinny, his arms were muscular.

"Honestly? I don't know that either. There might be some danger involved—for me, not for you—but I don't even know that for sure."

Ernie looked at him warily.

"It's a long story. They might be doing something illegal there, and I have to find out."

"You a cop or a PI?"

"No, just someone who got involved in something by

accident."

Chat didn't want another innocent person killed, so he said, "When we land, I'll give you the remainder of the money I owe you. I'll go check it out. If you feel uncomfortable or threatened at any time, you take off. Leave and forget you ever made the journey."

"How will you get out?"

And then it hit Chat like a ton of bricks.

"Honestly? I'm not sure I'm meant to."

*****

Ernie figured out the location based on the coordinates Chat gave him, and they landed in a remote valley shortly before noon.

"You sure this is it?" asked Ernie.

"I'm not sure of anything," answered Chat.

He reached into his pocket and handed Ernie $3000. He added another $500 for expenses.

"Thank you. I hope I'll be flying back with you, but as I said before, if you feel like you need to leave, go. Don't worry about me."

"Can't leave you way out here," said Ernie.

"I'll be fine. I don't have a whole lot to live for right now. I'm paying your bill, so if I say leave if you are uncomfortable, then leave. If you're still here and I haven't returned in a couple of hours, then leave. Don't worry about me."

"If you say so. I'll turn the plane around and be ready to take off."

Chat shook hands with Ernie and got out of the plane. He saw a wide trail going into the trees, so he headed for it. As soon as he entered the tree cover, the sun was gone. The forest had a spooky feel to it. He reached into his backpack and pulled out his revolver. The trail had branched off. He followed the part that had branched, only because it was wider. But it ended at a cliff wall. He backtracked and got on the second part of the trail. This one was narrower. He walked for a few more minutes, then saw a faint light.

He slowed his pace and got off the trail. Using trees for cover, he approached the light, then stopped.

There was a clearing. The light he saw was the sun shining into the clearing. At the edge of the clearing was a wooden shack. It was long—maybe fifty feet—but narrow. It couldn't have been more than fifteen feet wide.

They were storing weapons *here*?

The door opened, and a man stepped out. He wore a gray jumpsuit, like a warehouse worker would wear. He lit a cigarette and soaked up the little bit of sun.

The cigarette finished, he flicked it away and re-entered the building.

Chat was about to move when the door opened again, and two men emerged from the shack. One was a skinny man dressed in bland brown coat with a furry black hat covering the tops of his ears. Chat had seen those in movies. Russians always seemed to wear them.

The other man was big. Huge was more the word. He was well over six feet and broad in the body. He had to weigh at least 250 pounds.

Could it be?

Both men lit cigarettes. The skinny man asked a question in a foreign language. Chat was pretty sure it was Russian. The big man answered in a deep voice.

It was him! There was no doubt about it. It was the voice

he had heard in the bathroom.

It was the man they called The Russian.

Chapter 23

Chat couldn't believe it. The Russian was here. He could kill him right now.

Then, the door opened, and a man with a rifle stepped out. He was dressed in military fatigues. But Chat could tell that he wasn't regular military. Probably a mercenary hired to protect their project. How many of them were there? There couldn't be many. The building wasn't big enough. In fact, it wasn't big enough for any of this. Could it be that there was something below ground? It would make sense. Dickson referred to it as a bunker. Weren't bunkers usually below ground?

Chat sat against a tree out of sight from the building. What was he going to do?

He hadn't planned this very well. His hatred for everyone involved with this had blinded him to the particulars. He knew he had to kill The Russian. To do so, he'd probably have to kill the skinny man with him. He'd also have to deal with the military guy with the rifle and any of his friends. What about the others? The workers. Did he have to kill them, as well? How many of them were there?

Suddenly, Chat couldn't breathe, and his chest felt constricted. Was he having a heart attack? No, it was a panic attack. He'd had them before and knew the signs. He put his head between his knees and wrapped his arms around them. He had to let it pass, but he couldn't let anyone hear him gasping for breath.

Chat closed his eyes and thought of Nancy. Instead of creating hatred for The Russian, it calmed him down. He thought about them making love. It had been a nice night. *Concentrate on the night, Chat!*

Slowly, the panic subsided, and his breathing returned to normal. He lifted his head and breathed in the crisp air. The panic attack was over. He knew what he had to do.

They all had to die—even the workers. After all, they knew what they were doing. They weren't innocent in all this.

Once he came to that conclusion, Chat was suddenly calm. It might end badly for him, but he didn't care at this point. He was focused on his goal.

Chat looked over at the building. They had all gone back inside. Well, maybe. The guy with the rifle might still be outside checking the area. If so, Chat had to take care of him first.

But how? If he shot him, everyone would hear the gun. Chat would lose any element of surprise. How about a club? If he could get close enough to the man and hit him over the head with something heavy, it would put him out of commission. Chat would then have his revolver and the man's rifle—assuming he could figure out how it worked.

Chat looked around him for something heavy. A rock? The only problem with that would be that he'd have to get very close and might lose his element of surprise. A stick—one heavy enough to kill a man but not too heavy to swing.

There was nothing right around him, so he went back along the trail away from the building. There! Sitting right on the trail was the perfect weapon—a tree branch about the size of a short baseball bat. It even had a slightly thinner end that could be used as the handle to grip.

He picked it up and swung it—perfect! He hurried back to his hiding spot and waited. He wondered how long Ernie would wait for him to return before he left. He hadn't heard the plane leave, but would he? It was a long hike through the forest to the valley.

The door opened, and the man in fatigues walked down the steps, lighting a cigarette. He let his rifle hang by a strap and didn't appear worried about any enemies showing up. He walked around the building from the other side, eventually emerging next to the building on Chat's side. The man was still too far away for a sneak attack, so Chat waited. Finally, he turned toward the trail Chat had taken and decided to check it out. It would bring him within feet of Chat.

Hiding behind the tree, Chat waited. As the guard passed him, Chat swung the club. The man sensed the movement, but it was too late. Chat brought the club down hard on the man's head. He dropped to the ground like a rock.

Chat grabbed the man's shoulders and dragged him far into the woods. There, he checked him for a pulse. He was still alive!

Should he kill him?

Well, he was either all in or not.

He didn't want to club him again, so Chat closed the man's nose and held his hand over the man's mouth. The guard never woke up. After five minutes, Chat checked for a pulse. He was dead.

Chat lifted the man's rifle. It was heavier than he would have thought. It seemed to be some kind of machine gun. It looked easy enough to shoot, but it would be his weapon of last resort.

Chat carried the machine gun on his back by the strap and had the club in one hand and his revolver in the other. He headed for the building. Once there, he took a deep breath, walked up the steps, and pushed open the door.

The first person he encountered was The Russian's skinny friend. The man looked at him in surprise. He reached for a gun, and Chat shot him. The man staggered. The bullet hadn't killed him, so Chat swung the club and connected with his head. The crack was loud, and the man's head burst open. He was dead before he hit the floor.

The Russian had been sitting in a large chair in the far corner, and Chat hadn't seen him. Suddenly, a shot rang out, and a round whizzed past his head. The Russian was walking toward him, firing. Chat fired back and caught The Russian in the chest. Two more shots also found their marks, and The Russian fell.

No one else was in the room, and the building looked even smaller on the inside than it did on the outside. It was one large room. There had to be more than this.

Then he saw an open trapdoor in the floor. As he suspected, something was under the building. As he approached it, gunfire came from below and bullets flew through the hole. Chat waited for it to stop, then reached over and pulled the trigger on the machine gun. Using only one hand, he had little control over the gun, and bullets sprayed all over the room below.

He heard a scream. Then silence.

Chat looked down the hole. An armed man in military fatigues lay sprawled on the floor, blood seeping out of numerous gunshot wounds.

With the machine gun in front of him, Chat slowly made his way down the stairs. He confirmed that the one who had shot up through the trapdoor was dead. His machine gun was on the floor near him. The man in the gray jumpsuit he had seen outside was also there, leaning against the wall, bleeding from his leg.

"Where are the weapons?" asked Chat.

"Where ... you ... never ... find ...them," the man said in halting English.

He sneered at Chat, so Chat shot him. He dropped to the floor, and Chat felt for a pulse. Nothing.

The room was empty of any other people.

The man in the gray jumpsuit told him he would never find the weapons. Was it because they were no longer there? He didn't think so. The way the man said it told him the weapons were hidden somewhere.

The room he was in held a couple of long tables and a few chairs. Beyond that room were two tunnels. They had lights, but Chat had no desire to explore them. When he got back, he would give the FBI the coordinates of the place and let them know that there might be weapons there. He would do it all anonymously, of course.

Chat looked around at the dead guard and the other dead worker. He had no problem with the fact that he had just killed them. Neither of them was innocent.

He climbed the stairs to the upper building. It was time to go. Hopefully, Ernie was still waiting for him.

As he turned to leave, Chat felt a burning in his back and, at the same time, heard a gun go off.

He'd been shot.

He turned and felt another bullet strike his body, this time in the stomach.

He looked down to see the dying Russian lying on the floor, holding a pistol. He stared at Chat and cursed in Russian.

Chat lifted his revolver and pulled the trigger. It was a lucky shot, hitting The Russian in the forehead. The man was certainly dead now.

Chat suddenly couldn't feel his legs, and he dropped to the floor in a sitting position. The pain in his back was excruciating, but it was the blood pouring out of his stomach area that scared him. He leaned back against the door. Maybe with it closed, the animals wouldn't come in and rip him to shreds.

He was going to die. Of course, he was. Maybe he always knew he wasn't going to leave this place alive. Even if Ernie showed up, he could do nothing for Chat. He was going to die very soon.

He thought of Nancy and what could have been. He thought about *The Wonder Boys*. Where were their bodies? If only they hadn't come to Alaska.

If only…

*****

Ernie had already taken off. When he heard the first shots in the distance, he started the engine, headed down the valley, and was airborne in seconds.

Should he tell anyone? Chat said not to.

Chat had commented on getting involved in something that he regretted. If that were the case, then he would probably regret it too.

No, it was better to keep silent. And that's what he would do.

He would never tell anyone.

Never.

*****

The next day, a small plane landed in the valley. It was The Russian's plane. The pilot waited an hour for The Russian to appear. When no movement came from the forest, the pilot left the plane and walked down the trail.

When the plane with the band went down, The Russian knew he had to complete the arms deal on his own. So he had come out with a small group of men. The sellers were a nervous group and opened fire on The Russian and his men, killing one. That infuriated his boss. The deal was off. The Russian's men dealt with the sellers quickly, disposing of their bodies in the forest. The pilot knew it wasn't the way The Russian liked to do business, but he was provoked.

The Russian had lost a million dollars when the plane with his man disappeared. But by killing the sellers, he had saved the second million. His boss was satisfied. He told the pilot to return in two days, after his boss had taken an inventory of the weapons.

As he approached the building, the pilot slowed. Something was wrong. He didn't know what, but he could feel it. He pulled out his pistol.

The pilot slowly opened the door and glanced in. He had to push on the door, as something was blocking it. Some*one*. A man lay dead in front of it. The smell of dead bodies was the first thing to hit him. It was overwhelming. He almost turned and ran, but he had to make sure his boss wasn't alive. He squeezed past the man blocking the door. The next person he saw was Viktor, his boss's right-hand man. The pilot didn't like Viktor and wasn't sad to see him dead. But if he was dead, then…

There he was. His boss. He was sprawled on his stomach. His huge frame suddenly seemed small on the floor. There was blood all around him and a bullet hole in his forehead.

The pilot shivered. The hatch to the maze of rooms below was open. He slowly crept down the stairs. The minute he saw the two bodies, he knew it was time to leave. Everyone was dead.

What about the weapons? Were they still there?

He didn't care. It was none of his business. He didn't care what had happened to them. All he knew was that he was out of a job. He could fly back and tell The Russian's son that his father was dead, but then what? He didn't want to work for the boy they called The Ghost. The boy was volatile and might take his anger out on him. No, he'd fly back to Anchorage and get lost. Maybe he'd begin a new life in Canada somewhere. He started out the door, then stopped.

His employer always carried a lot of cash with him. He wouldn't need it now. The pilot went over to the dead man and found his wallet—a large purse attached to a chain. He unzipped it and removed the cash.

There were hundreds of dollars! Maybe a few thousand. He checked Viktor's wallet and pulled out several hundred dollars.

He stuffed the money in his pocket and left the building, stepping over the man by the door, then pulling the door closed behind him. He ran all the way to his plane and started the engines.

He looked around. He wasn't going to miss this place.

As the plane took off, he wondered what had become of the cache of weapons. He didn't care, just as he didn't care about this remote place. He had heard of Dickson's death, so to his knowledge, he was the only one left who knew anything about the operation.

    And he wasn't about to tell anyone—ever!

Chapter 24

ALASKA—2010

The woman walked through the forest. Was there once a trail here? Maybe. At times, she saw spots that indicated an old trail. But for the most part, it was all overgrown.

She was an experienced pilot who had flown herself here in a small, single-engine plane.

This was going to be her last assignment. They knew it. Maybe it's why she was given such an unpleasant task.

Natalya had no choice but to leave. She had just found out she was pregnant. The pregnancy was a mistake—just one of those careless moments. The father of the child—her husband—was also a mistake—another careless decision. She didn't want a child of hers growing up with him as the father. She had to leave the organization to take care of her baby.

As bad of a reputation as the KGB had—and most of it was warranted—they weren't giving her an overly hard time about retiring at the ripe old age of twenty-nine. They didn't like it, and they let her know. They were pissed at having spent so much money training her. But it wasn't unprecedented. Many female agents had retired when they became pregnant. Others continued in the job even after having children, but it rarely worked out well for them or the children.

Natalya was beginning to wonder if her final assignment would be a bust. After all, it was just a rumor, and rumors were notoriously inaccurate.

The bunkers had been rumored for years. They were supposed to hold munitions to begin the takeover of America. Rumors—that's all they were. But this one was different. It didn't just hold munitions; it held a very powerful and very dangerous shipment that had been stolen from the U.S. military.

A large shipment had vanished—that part was true. And the suspected arms dealer had also vanished, never to be seen again. That was also true. The arms dealer was both famous and unknown at the same time. He really existed and was responsible for countless arms deals. But no one knew anything about him. Now, she was following the story told by an ex-pilot on his deathbed about a secret bunker out in the middle of nowhere. The man supposedly worked for the arms dealer. By the time he told the story, he was senile and close to death. No one really believed him, but she was sent to verify that the story was his imagination. After all, he was very specific about the location. An easy last assignment? No. More like a punishment for quitting. Stick her where no one else wanted to go.

Their attitude pissed her off. She had done an excellent job for them. She was a standout operative. No one knew that the quiet woman from Seattle was a deadly assassin.

Bits of the trail kept popping up, so she continued in the same direction. Finally, she arrived at a partial clearing—just enough of an opening in the trees to let a little sun through.

There it was. A cabin. It was run down, but it was there, just as the pilot had said it was.

Natalya approached it slowly. She pulled out her weapon but knew it wouldn't be needed unless an unfriendly animal had made his home in the shack.

She opened the door carefully and turned on her flashlight. She immediately saw skeletons—bones inside ragged clothes. One of the skeletons had been lying next to the door. There was nothing else in the rectangular cabin—except an open trapdoor.

She shined her light down the hole and then proceeded to climb down the stairs, shining her flashlight all around as she descended to make sure she wouldn't be surprised. She reached the bottom and looked around.

Two more sets of bones.

Natalya looked around the room. It was empty except for a couple of tables and some chairs. Shining her flashlight, she saw two tunnels.

She walked down one of them. There were rooms on each side, but all were empty. Following the tunnel, it wound around and eventually led back to the main room under the trapdoor. It wasn't two tunnels but one continuous tunnel with two entrances. Other than a few bedrooms, the other rooms were all empty of anything but junk. There was no evidence of munitions. Whatever might have once been there wasn't there now.

Natalya took a last look around, then climbed the ladder. She left through the only door and took a breath of air. She was an experienced agent and was embarrassed that she had found it all rather spooky.

She spent a few minutes walking around the building, then decided that what she was sent to find wasn't there. All she saw were the remnants of ventilation tubes coming from the sleeping quarters.

Had munitions—including the special ones—ever been

stored there? Once upon a time, they probably had. But she was many years too late to find anything of value.

Natalya would go back and tell them that she didn't find anything. It wasn't exactly a lie. She didn't find what they were looking for. She just found a building with a lot of old skeletons. There were no munitions. If they were there at one time, they probably had already shipped them out somewhere before everyone died.

How did they die? It was an interesting question but one that was meaningless at this point. Did they ship out the munitions and were killed? Did someone kill them and steal the munitions?

Curiosity got the best of her, and she re-entered the building. That's when she noticed the guns under piles of dust and debris. One of the skeletons had a hole in the skull. There had been a gunfight. Her curiosity was satisfied. She left the building, closing the door behind her.

She tromped through the heavy underbrush back to the plane, an anticlimactic end to a short but productive career.

There was no need to tell them that she had found the skeletons. The important thing was that there were no munitions. So screw 'em, as the Americans said. She would go to her home in Seattle to live. Once upon a time, it was part of her cover. Now, it would be her legitimate home. There, she would find a quiet job and raise her child. Although it was too early to determine the sex, she knew in her heart that it was a girl. She already had a name picked out. It was her grandmother's name, although she would change the spelling to make it more palatable for Americans. It was a nice name—a gentle name.

Michaela.

THE 7TH PASSENGER

PART THREE

PRESENT DAY

Chapter 25

"Was it him?" asked one of the quasi-military men on the ground.

Scott's plane had flown over for the third or fourth time.

"It's him," answered Gwen Slade. "He didn't take my advice to leave us alone."

"You threatened to hurt his kid," said the man, the second-in-command. "Would you really?"

"How? We don't have the numbers to do something like that. There are four of us. I can't spare anyone for that kind of job. Besides, he's the only one we've seen, so I doubt he's told anyone. He's just an idiot doing it on his own. I don't know what he expects to find."

"Here he comes again."

"See if you can get a clear shot," said Slade. "Maybe we won't have to worry about him if he crashes."

As the plane flew over, gunshots erupted, then quickly stopped.

"I hit it!" shouted one of the men.

"He's climbing," said the woman. "You may have hit him, but I don't think it did any damage."

The plane wasn't returning.

"I think we scared him off," said one of the men. "What

now?"

"We have to do this quickly," Slade said. "We can't have him tell anyone."

"Are you sure it's here?" asked her second-in-command.

"That's the word we got. They said it was well hidden, and it's not in the bunker. So it has to be buried."

"We've gone over acres with the metal detectors," said the man.

"And we'll go over as many acres as we have to. A metal detector might not find them if housed in concrete or a lead box."

"Then how the hell are we supposed to find it?"

"Just keep looking. Continue to look for anomalies in the landscape—hills that don't look real or depressions in the ground that could hide a door."

But she knew that it was a fruitless search. The man made a good point: The metal detectors were useless if the object wasn't housed in something metal. Frankly, the whole mission was futile. But she was being paid to look, which is what she was doing.

However, two days later, they were ready to give up. They had tested the ground for hard areas under the surface that might indicate storage bins, but they only found rocks. They searched at least a mile in each direction for rock formations that could indicate something stored below.

Finally, the woman put a halt to it.

"This is ridiculous," she said. "Our esteemed employer"—she made a face as she said it—"has got to realize that someone got to those munitions a long time ago. It's probably why they all died in there. They were killed, and whoever killed them stole the weapons. I tried to explain that to him before, but he will have to accept it."

There was a noise from the trees, and all four turned toward it.

A shot rang out, and one of the men dropped to the ground. As the others reached for weapons, more shots followed. One by one, they fell.

Lying in the dirt, Slade could feel her life slipping away from a neck wound. She watched as a group of six men entered the clearing. With them was a girl.

It was the girl from the plane!

The woman's eyes closed. Seconds later, she was dead.

Chapter 26

Alexander Petrov was suddenly a man in great demand. He had recently retired from the KGB and bought a home near the Black Sea. He had a private beach and a 40-foot boat.

He also had a lot of debt.

Purchasing the home and the boat and dealing with the upkeep had been more expensive than he'd imagined. So, when he was approached one day by Prescott's man, Hagen, and asked if he had ever heard of a place in Alaska nicknamed "the bunker," he knew he had found his means to get out of debt.

Alexander had almost forgotten the final mission he had sent Natalya on—to find the bunker. Once she let him know that the bunker was empty of weapons, he put it out of his mind. But when Hagen approached him, he quickly searched through his records until he found the coordinates he had passed on to Natalya.

He demanded a premium price for the information, and almost got it. But the amount he settled for was still enough to get him out of debt.

That got him thinking. If Prescott was willing to pay so much, what would the world's covert agencies be willing to spend? He soon found out. He'd never promised any of the groups exclusivity to the information. The CIA and Mossad jumped at the opportunity to finally locate the mythical "bunker," and paid a small fortune for the information. MI-6 balked at the price for something that might not even exist. The KGB, who had provided him with the information in the first place, but had then lost it, wanted the information for free, seeing as how he was their former agent. He couldn't refuse them. Out of a sense of loyalty, he let them know that Natalya hadn't found any weapons. However, they wanted the location of former agent Natalya Orlova, or, to be more precise, the location of the dead agent's daughter.

Alexander knew nothing about the missing weapons, but he did know where Natalya's daughter was. Alexander and Natalya had a cordial relationship when she worked for him and maintained contact for a few years after she retired. Part of that was a requirement by the KGB, and part was his interest in her life once her career ended.

He knew that she had given birth to a girl and that she named her Michaela. He followed her from afar as she began her post-spying life in Seattle and later moved to Anchorage. Alexander was saddened when he learned that she had died of cancer but happy that Michaela had ended up being adopted by a man in Alaska.

When the KGB demanded to know where the girl lived, he was compelled to give it to them.

The KGB already knew the location of the bunker, since he was the one who had told them. But why did they want the girl? Of course! They wanted Natalya's papers. They must have felt that Natalya knew more than she had let on. And maybe she did. He had always suspected that she had found something there. Maybe not the weapons, but something.

Alexander could only imagine the stampede of operatives

or contractors heading to Alaska. But he didn't care. He got his money.

And that was all that mattered.

Chapter 27

It was nice having a friend. Michaela couldn't remember the last time she had a good friend. When she lived with her mother, she had a lot of school buddies, but not a close friend since third grade—and that girl moved away. After that, Michaela kept to herself, much to her mother's concern.

Sally was fun to be with and smart. She also wasn't into a lot of the wilder things that a lot of the kids were.

Michaela hadn't told Sally about her adventures of a few months earlier, but word had gotten out. Sally had asked her a few questions, but Michaela kept her answers general. The last thing Michaela wanted was for Sally to find out that she had killed people. It might scare her off. Then again, Sally seemed to be mature enough to accept it. But Michaela wasn't ready to take that chance. Later, maybe when they had known each other longer.

Sally knew about Michaela's mom dying and Scott adopting her. But again, Michaela chose to keep most of the details private. Even when Sally asked, Michaela didn't tell her about her biological father—a man who had a plan to potentially kill thousands of people. Sally had become a good friend, but what if they had a falling out? Would Sally tell everyone what she knew about Michaela's past? Probably not, but keeping most of it private was still better.

They had finished their project early for the day and decided to walk into town to grab a slice of pizza. Scott had a client to take over to the town of Seldovia, across the bay. It wasn't a long flight, but he would get home too late to pick up Michaela, so they arranged for Jess to pick her up.

Michaela called Jess and told her their plans and that she could pick her up in an hour at the pizza parlor. Sally did the same with her parents.

Remembering what Scott told her, Michaela was aware of her surroundings and made sure she wasn't being followed. But she also remembered Scott saying that Special Agent Briggs thought it was unlikely that the people Scott saw would really send anyone to harm her.

Just as they reached the pizza parlor, Michaela's phone rang.

"It's Scott's SAT phone," she said. "He's probably calling from his plane. You go on in and I'll be in in a minute."

"Okay. Take your time."

Sally went in as Michaela answered.

"Hi, Scott."

At that moment, two men—one on each side of her—suddenly appeared almost out of nowhere. Each took one of her arms and lifted her a few inches off the ground. One of the men grabbed her cell phone while the other clapped his hand over her mouth. They turned the corner of the building, which led to a small parking lot behind the pizza parlor. With Michaela immobilized, they stepped into an unmarked blue van and shut the door.

Michaela's eyes were wide with fear. The man who had taken her phone pulled something out of a box—a needle!

Michaela tried to struggle, but she was being held too

tightly. She felt a sharp pain in her arm and immediately felt dizzy.

What was happening?

She suddenly became very drowsy. She looked at the men who had taken her. In the gloom of the back of the van, she saw that both men were blonde and large. Neither had said a word.

Why were they taking her—and where?

Those were her last thoughts before she lost consciousness.

*****

Sally found a seat and looked out the window. Where was Michaela? That was strange. She was right behind her. If it had been an emergency call, Michaela would have told her. Sally got up from the seat and went to the door. Nothing.

She walked outside and looked up and down the street. There was no sign of Michaela.

Sally wasn't worried—yet. Maybe it was an emergency, and Michaela didn't even have time to tell her. But that was so unlike Michaela. She was one of the most responsible kids she had ever known. Maybe that's why they connected so easily—neither had much use for the stupid things that so many others in their class did.

And it wasn't that Michaela and Sally were too serious to have fun. They loved to have fun—just not juvenile stuff.

Sally stood in the doorway. A blue van pulled out of the parking lot behind the pizza parlor and headed down the road. A few people were walking on the sidewalk, but there was nothing out of the ordinary—except no Michaela.

She should go in and get a slice of pizza and wait for Michaela. But Sally couldn't eat now. In her gut, she knew something was wrong.

She tried Michaela's phone, but it went directly to voicemail like it had been turned off.

Sally looked at her watch. It would still be another 45 minutes before Jess came to pick up Michaela. She suddenly wished she had Jess's phone number. She didn't even have Michaela's adoptive father's number. Scott was his name. She was just going to have to wait.

Should she call the police? What would she tell them? No, better to wait for Jess. She would know what to do. After all, Jess was famous for her role in the Wisdom Spring affair. She was especially famous in Homer, since some of the action had happened there.

Forty minutes passed. Sally's mother showed up, but Sally told her they'd have to wait—something had happened to Michaela.

A minute later, Jess pulled up.

"What's wrong?" she asked. She could see it in Sally's face.

"I don't know." Sally began to cry. "Michaela was right behind me. Just as we were going in, her phone rang. She said she'd meet me inside. I heard her say 'Hi, Scott.' I went in and sat down. When I looked out the window, she was gone. I went outside. She disappeared. I'm sorry I didn't call the police, but I didn't know what to do. I hoped you would."

Sally's mother hugged her, and Jess said, "There's nothing for you to be sorry about. We don't know yet what happened."

"What if she was kidnapped?" asked Sally, tears running down her face.

"Let's not jump to conclusions," said her mother.

But Jess knew that it was exactly what happened. And whoever did it was a professional, otherwise, Michaela would have put up a fight.

She looked at her watch. Scott should be back from Seldovia by now. She pulled out her phone.

This was a call she didn't want to make.

Chapter 28

I hung up the phone, and a chill went through my body. I was still at the airport, having just returned from the Seldovia trip.

They did it. They actually did it. They'd made good on their promise.

I knew it was them—the people who shot at us. It had to be. I mean, who else had a motive to take Michaela? It wasn't some pervert. I knew Michaela well enough to know that she would scream bloody murder and probably hurt the guy in the process.

No, this was quick and professional.

Briggs had dismissed the idea of those people actually following through on their threats. But I couldn't blame him. It didn't make sense to me, either. I could now dismiss the theory that they were poachers. This was way beyond poaching.

I suspected something was wrong when the connection was lost and she didn't call me back. And when I tried, it went to voicemail. I hoped it was just a bad connection, but somehow I knew.

I started to dial Brigg's number, then stopped. No, it was too early for that. I had to figure out what was going on first, and I had to know what they wanted.

Instead, I got in my truck and headed downtown to the

pizza parlor. When I got there, Sally and her mother were still there. Sally was in tears. I introduced myself to them.

Jess greeted me with a hug.

"I asked Sally if she had seen anything out of the ordinary, and she said she hadn't," Jess said.

"She was there one minute and gone the next," said Sally. "I should have paid more attention."

"It's not your fault," I said. "Michaela is pretty skilled for her age. If she could have, she would have made a racket. This was something different. And you saw nothing strange?"

"No. A blue van pulled out of the parking lot while I looked for her, but other than..."

"A van?" I asked, interrupting her. Kidnap victims always seemed to be put in vans.

"An old blue one," said Sally. "Is that helpful?"

"It might be. Which way did it go?"

"To the right. Like it was going through town."

I had seen that van!

"Thank you, Sally. Please don't worry about Michaela. I'm sure she's going to be fine."

I wasn't sure she would, but I couldn't tell Sally that. She was feeling bad enough as it was.

As Sally and her mother drove away, I told Jess, "I think I saw that van parked in the airport parking lot. I know most of the cars that park there daily, but I've never seen that one. And if they drove through town, that would lead them right to the airport."

I told Jess to go home and that I'd check out the airport. She said she'd fill Jon in on the situation.

I had a reason for wanting to go alone. It gave me the time to beat myself up. I was feeling terrible. It was all my fault that Michaela was taken. If anything happened to her, my life would be over. It was stupid of me to buzz them the day after the encounter Jon and I had with them. There was no good reason for me to do it. It was childish and stupid.

So, I spent the next ten minutes berating myself for being such an idiot. Once I reached the airport, though, I had put all that behind me. The job now was to find Michaela.

Homer Airport wasn't exactly a hub of activity. Like most small airports, it had no tower with air traffic controllers. It had one runway and one small terminal, so getting information on a particular plane might be possible. If anyone knew, it would be my buddy Sam.

Sam was sort of a jack-of-all-trades. He did anything that needed doing there, and he seemed to always be around. I found him fueling up a small plane.

"Hey, Sam," I said as I approached.

"Hey, Scott. Back so soon?"

"Yeah. You see everything around here, so I'm hoping you can answer some questions."

"Shoot."

"There's a blue van in the parking lot. Did you happen to see who it belongs to?"

"Nah. It wasn't there this morning. We did have a car stolen from the parking lot today. Can you believe it?"

"Right before I landed, did another plane take off? Maybe a plane you haven't seen before?"

"As a matter of fact, yes. It landed earlier today, and two men got out. A little while ago, the same two got back in the plane and took off. This time, they had someone with them—a female, I think. She might have been sick or drunk. The two guys were holding her up. You flew in about ten minutes after they took off."

It immediately made sense. Whoever landed stole a car

from the parking lot, drove into town, and stole the blue van. That was the van they used to kidnap Michaela, and the van Sally saw. And I missed them by ten minutes!

I thanked Sam and drove home, where Jon and Jess were waiting for me. I explained what I found.

"And you think it was the people we ran into?" asked Jon.

"Who else could it be? They specifically threatened to hurt Michaela."

"We need to contact Briggs," said Jon.

"I know. But my gut tells me to wait."

At that moment, my phone rang. No number showed up.

We all looked at each other. Could it be?

"Hello?"

"Scott…"

It was Michaela. She sounded drugged.

A different voice came on the phone. It was a male with a strong accent.

"Do you want to see your daughter alive?"

"Stupid question. Of course."

"Then you will do something for us."

Chapter 29

Prescott pressed the End Call on his phone for about the tenth time.

Something had happened. Slade wasn't answering her phone. There was only one reason for that—the woman was dead. The KGB contractors must have arrived and killed Slade and her team. If so, that was too bad. She was a valuable employee.

"What now?" asked Hagen.

Prescott set the phone down on his desk and looked at Hagen. While Slade was his most valuable field operative, Hagen was his right-hand man regarding his business. The man was brilliant with numbers and negotiations.

"I don't know," said Prescott. "Your man, Alexander, really screwed us over. We paid him a lot of money for the location of the site."

"He's not 'my man.' If anything, he's your man."

Hagen wasn't about to take the blame for this. Alexander was a contact Prescott had used several times before. Hagen's only relationship to the man was as Prescott's go-between.

"Yeah, I know," admitted Prescott. "But I'm never using him again."

"I'm guessing he just made a lot of money selling this

information. For all we know, he's now out of the business and enjoying life in his chalet by the beach," said Hagen. "Could it be time to call it quits on this one? We've spent a lot of money and time and are no closer to finding it than we were a few years ago."

"A few years ago, we didn't have a location," said Prescott. "Now we do."

"And now, so does everyone else," said Hagen. "What if one of the other groups has already located it?"

"You know as well as I do that we would have heard. We know everything that's going on in this industry."

"Not if they've just discovered it. After all, you just lost contact with Slade. If someone found it, they could still be there."

Prescott stared into space for a full minute before speaking.

"I might have to break my own rule and visit the site."

Hagen's mouth dropped open. It was a hard and fast rule that Prescott—or "The Ghost"—only negotiated over the phone. He had people to do the field work.

"Do you have any clue what some countries in need would pay for this?" Prescott asked. "Of course you do. Get one small country that wants to take over another small country, and these weapons would tip the balance in their favor. And they would pay mightily for this shipment. I would get more for this than I would if I sold a large nuclear weapon to a superpower. It's supply and demand, and this is in demand."

"Still, are you sure this is the best move? You don't know what would be waiting for you up there."

"We'll bring a team."

"We?" asked Hagen.

"I need you along."

"Okay."

What else could he say? The last thing Hagen wanted to do was to go to Alaska and visit this site. Hagen was a money man, but sometimes you had to see beyond the money. This was one of those times. It was a moot point because Prescott couldn't see it.

Hagen had worked for Prescott for over twenty years. Now in his late seventies, Prescott could have retired years ago. He was also a billionaire, but due to the nature of his business, you'd never see his name on a Forbes list. Prescott was good-looking and in great health for a man of his age. He should have been retired and enjoying his money, but he wasn't. His need to make more money was almost a disease. However, the money was only one aspect of the man.

In a rare alcohol-fueled moment many years before—a celebration after a huge arms sale—Prescott had opened up to Hagen and had talked about life with his father, The Russian. His father was a man even more driven by money than Prescott was. He was also a hard, vindictive man and a horrible father. He put tremendous pressure on his son to be just like him and to follow in his footsteps.

As much as Prescott hated his father, he had become just like him. It was the reason he never married or—God forbid—had a child. He knew what he was, and unlike his father, he didn't want to pass it on to anyone else.

And with all his money, Prescott was tightlipped about what would happen to it when he died. Hagen knew that a large sum was coming his way. Slade would've also benefitted if she wasn't dead. But who knew what would happen to the rest of it?

The fact was, Hagen didn't care, because he would never live to see any money. He had recently been diagnosed with liver cancer. There was nothing they could do about it. He was beginning to feel the pain, but it hadn't reached the unbearable stage yet. Even though Hagen had lost weight and was starting to look gaunt, Prescott hadn't noticed it. Prescott didn't notice things like that. He didn't know, and Hagen wouldn't tell him.

The reason? He hated the man.

Hagen had been an Explosive Ordnance Disposal Specialist in the Army—one of those people who defused bombs for a living. He was good at it, but the EOD stress finally got to him. An acquaintance introduced him to Prescott, who was looking for someone who knew weapons inside and out. In the process, Prescott also discovered that Hagen had negotiating skills and financial prowess. One thing led to another, and Hagen became integral to The Ghost's arms-dealing empire.

That was all well and good, but it didn't stop Prescott from being nasty and vindictive. On one hand, he valued Hagen's expertise, but on the other, he made it clear to Hagen who the boss was. Hagen was often belittled and emotionally castrated by the man.

About ten years into Prescott's employ, Hagen realized that he held the position for life. Meaning, of course, that he couldn't leave even if he wanted to—ever. And he definitely wanted to. Prescott would have him killed if he tried. Hagen no longer even liked dealing with munitions. He was just tired of it all.

So, at the ripe old age of forty-five, Hagen was going to die. He was no longer afraid of what Prescott could do to him. Prescott couldn't do anything that his body wasn't already doing.

Hagen had received the news about his cancer a month earlier. The news hit him hard, sending him into an emotional tailspin. He wanted to get back at somebody for his situation. And he had the perfect target—Prescott.

Within days, he was already plotting how to repay Prescott for all the misery the man had caused him. He secretly moved some of Prescott's offshore money into investments that were sure losers. He was still contemplating more severe actions when this trip came up. Suddenly, he realized the trip might be the perfect way to exact his revenge on his boss.

Prescott had let Hagen take over all of the finances. As a result, Hagen knew where every cent of Prescott's fortune was located. Because of that, he had one more thing to do that would put the final blow on Prescott's financial empire. He would put it into motion just as they were leaving, so if Prescott managed to survive this trip, he would return to an empty bank account.

But if Hagen had his way, Prescott wouldn't return from Alaska. What would the revenge be in Alaska? He didn't know yet. But he was an intelligent guy. He would see the opportunity when it presented itself. He might die in the process, but at this point, it didn't matter.

What mattered was that he would see Prescott pay.

Chapter 30

Michaela woke up with a massive headache.

She was in something that was moving, and it was loud. A plane!

Michaela was lying on the floor. She tried to move, but her wrists were tied, and she was dizzy—so dizzy. Suddenly, she threw up.

They hit a moment of turbulence, and she rolled right into her vomit, covering one side of her face. The smell made her vomit a second time.

A man laughed and said something to another person. It was in Russian. Michaela, having grown up with a Russian mother, spoke the language. The man had said how gross Michaela looked with vomit on her face.

She was about to say something but stopped. Do they know she speaks Russian? Probably not. It would be best not to reveal that fact. She needed to learn as much from them as she could.

One of the men asked her jokingly if she was comfortable. Michaela pretended not to understand. So, he said in English, "You had a Russian mother, but you don't know the language? Stupid girl."

Michaela thought back to her ordeal a few months earlier.

Someone called her a stupid girl then, as well. That person was now dead. Maybe this man would follow the same course.

Michaela chose not to reply. She was beginning to think more clearly. She remembered the phone call and then the needle in her arm. They had drugged her!

And then she thought of the man's comment. How did he know that her mother was Russian?

Then her thoughts flashed to Scott. How was he going to react to her being taken? She knew. He'd go ballistic. He'd call in the Marines to get her. But the Marines Scott would call wouldn't be part of the military. He'd get Jon and their friend Joe. Joe had some kind of secret background. She couldn't remember exactly, but she thought it was the CIA. She just knew from firsthand experience that he was deadly when he had to be.

Scott had other friends, as well. Michaela had gone with Scott when he had to deliver some packages to a community on Piney Lake. Scott called them a survivalist community. He told her that they had helped him in the Wisdom Spring affair. She had met them. A really tough crowd, but they always treated her with courtesy and respect.

Her mind was clearing, but nothing made sense. Why did they take her? Scott had warned her about the people who shot at him and threatened to do something to her. But she was sure that Scott said they sounded American. These men were Russian. Were they part of the same group Scott ran across? The whole thing was confusing, but adding the Russians to the mix made it stranger.

"Little girl, I'm talking to you!"

Michaela had been so deep in her thoughts that she hadn't heard the man speaking.

"Sorry," she replied. "I'm a little foggy."

She wasn't, but they didn't have to know that.

"Sit up."

Michaela struggled to get up into a sitting position on the plane's floor.

"Do you have your mother's things?" he asked.

"My mother's things?" asked Michaela. "What things? I don't understand."

And she didn't understand. Why would he be asking her that question?

"Your dead mother's belongings."

Using the term "dead mother" was like a gut punch for Michaela. Tears formed, and suddenly she was crying.

"Stop crying!"

But she couldn't. The combination of being kidnapped and being reminded that her mother was dead was too much to handle. The crying increased.

"I said, stop crying."

The man slapped her, and Michaela fell over, crying out in pain. She heard one of the men tell her abuser in Russian to stop and to give her time to compose herself.

Michaela looked up at the one who had hit her. He wasn't one of the two who had taken her. They were blonde. This man had a shaved head and a two-inch scar on his chin. She wouldn't forget him. If she ever got the chance, he would be the one she would kill.

"Sit up," said one of the other men gently.

Michaela had seen enough cop shows. They were doing the good cop/bad cop routine on her. Well, it wouldn't work!

She slowly pushed herself back to a sitting position. The tears had stopped, but her face still stung from the slap.

"I asked you a question," the bald man said, now in a less commanding tone.

"I don't understand what you mean," replied Michaela. "I have boxes of her things—clothes, pictures, and personal things, but…"

"Do you have her papers?" he asked, interrupting her.

"Papers? Some of them, I guess. I didn't pay much attention to the papers. I just put them in boxes."

"And where are those boxes? Are they at Scott Harper's house?"

What could she say? If she said yes, it would put Scott in danger. If she said no, they would know she was lying. Either way, Scott wasn't safe.

"Yes," she finally said, having no choice.

"Good," was all the man said. He went back to sit with the others.

A few minutes later, they landed. Michaela recognized it as the same valley she and Scott had landed in. It wasn't the second valley that Scott had told her about.

When the plane stopped, the bald man pulled out a large phone. Michaela recognized it as a satellite phone. He dialed a number, then held the phone near Michaela's ear, so he and the others could also hear.

"Hello?"

"Scott…"

The man took the phone away.

"Do you want to see your daughter alive?"

Scott said something on the other end.

"Then you will do something for us. Your daughter has boxes with her mother's things. You will collect those boxes and load them onto your plane. You will then fly them to a landing strip. Here are the coordinates."

The man didn't know that Michaela and Scott had already been there.

Michaela could faintly hear Scott now.

"They are all in a storage locker, and the facility is closed for the day. I can't get to them until tomorrow, and it's a whole houseful of boxes. It's a lot of boxes to load onto my plane."

Michaela knew that neither of those statements was true.

"Your daughter says they are at your house."

"She's wrong. I moved everything to a storage locker. I didn't have the room to store it all."

The man looked doubtful, then said, "Okay. But you'll do it?"

"Of course I will, but what are you looking for? It might save me some time."

"It's none of your business."

"It'll probably take most of the day, and I don't want to fly up there at night."

The three Russians looked at each other. The bald one said in Russian, "Should we give him the day?" The others nodded.

"You have tomorrow to find the boxes. Then we expect you to fly up here the morning of the next day. Is that clear?"

Michaela couldn't hear Scott's response, but she assumed that he agreed.

"One more thing," said the bald one. "You are not to call the authorities, or your daughter will die. If you've already called them, call them back and tell them that you found her."

"I haven't called them," Michaela heard Scott say.

"Good. Keep it that way. I will call you tomorrow night. And Scott Harper, don't fail us."

He smiled at his friends.

"Or your daughter will die a very slow and very painful death."

Chapter 31

After the bald man hung up with Scott, he ushered Michaela off the plane. A second plane was sitting near the trees, and two other men were waiting for them.

"Where are we going," asked Michaela as she tried to rub the dried vomit off her face with her sleeve.

"You'll see," said the bald man.

"I don't understand. Why do you want my mother's papers? If you're looking for the logbook, you're too late."

The man stopped and grabbed her arm.

"What logbook?"

"It was a logbook written by a Russian sailor long ago, leading to some treasure. The treasure has already been found."

Michaela thought back a few months to her adventure with Scott in the wilderness. The logbook played a significant part in it.

The Russian let go of her arm and continued walking.

"We're not looking for an ancient logbook."

Then he stopped again and stared incredulously at Michaela.

"You really don't know?"

"Know what?"

"About your mother? Who your mother was?"

Michaela shivered.

"She was my mother. That's all she was."

"That's not all she was. Your mother was a spy for the KGB."

"Bullshit!" yelled Michaela. "You're so stupid! You've got the wrong person. My mother wasn't a spy."

She didn't even see the slap coming. The bald man struck her so hard, she landed on the ground and rolled almost five feet. It hurt worse than the first one, and she screamed in pain. This time, she began to sob uncontrollably. One of the other men came over to pick her up, and she slapped his arm away.

She was crying for two reasons. The first was from the intense pain. The second was the realization that the man was right, and it answered some questions she'd always had about her mother—secret phone calls, telling people on the phone to leave her alone, and once when Michaela overheard her say in Russian, "I don't do that anymore." When Michaela asked about her comment, her mother refused to talk about it.

The man who tried to help her up a moment earlier grabbed her arm and not so gently pulled her to her feet.

"Move," he commanded.

They walked for another half hour; then the bald man raised a fist for them to stop.

"Do not say a word," he whispered to Michaela.

She nodded. What were they doing? Then she heard voices—a woman and at least a couple of men. They sounded American.

It all happened quickly. Her group emerged from the trees and immediately started firing. There were three men and a woman. Seconds later, all four were sprawled on the ground dead. The Russians moved on as if nothing happened.

A few minutes later, they arrived at a clearing—or what had once been a clearing. Now, it was an area overgrown with bushes and shrubs, surrounded by the forest. A small rundown wooden building sat at the edge of the clearing. Two tents had been set up near the building in an area cleared of brush. One tent had three cots, and the other had a single cot and boxes of food and water. Michaela assumed the woman had stayed in the tent with the single cot. She figured the men would put her there, but no, they led her into the building.

The first thing she saw were three skeletons. She shook her head in amazement. It seemed that all she ever encountered were skeletons.

Two of the men climbed down through a trapdoor and were gone for several minutes. When they came up, they said to the others in Russian that it was all clear.

"There's a room for the girl, too."

Was she going to be stuck underground?

She balked when they pushed her toward the hole.

"Don't make us hurt you," said the bald man. "Now, go!"

Michaela carefully climbed down the ladder. It was dark, but one of the men turned on a battery-powered lantern. He found two more and turned them on, illuminating a large room—and two more skeletons.

The man grabbed Michaela's arm and pulled her down a narrow hallway. They came to a door, and he pushed Michaela in and set a lantern on the floor.

"Your room," he said in Russian.

The room had two sets of bunk beds with just the bare mattresses. In the middle of the room, there was also a folding table and two chairs.

Michaela pretended not to understand, so the man called to one of the others. The bald man entered the room and said, "He says this is your room."

"It's cold, and I have to pee."

The bald man told the other in Russian to bring her a bucket, some toilet paper, and a blanket from one of the tents.

When the man left, the bald one said to her, "You're pathetic, not even knowing your native language."

Michaela wanted to say that her native language was English, but that would be risking another slap, so she said nothing.

A few minutes later, the other man brought a blanket, a bucket, a bottle of water, and a Meal-Ready-to-Eat. The MRE was appreciated, as she was starving.

Without another word, they left the room and closed the door. The room didn't have a lock, but there was no way Michaela could sneak out without being seen, so a lock wasn't necessary.

She didn't really have to pee, but she knew she would soon. The idea of peeing in an open bucket disgusted her. And then, what would happen when she had to poop? She couldn't think about it.

The thought of sitting on one of the dirty old mattresses was gross, so Michaela sat on the floor and ate her meal. It was some kind of chicken and rice dinner, but she barely tasted it. She was thinking about Scott. Would he find her? What if he brought them the boxes they wanted? They would never let him live. Scott had to know that.

She just hoped he had a plan.

Chapter 32

I was shaking as I put my phone down on the kitchen table. I felt lightheaded, so I sat on one of the kitchen chairs. I knew the coordinates he had given me. They were of the landing strip I had used three times already.

What was going on? I had eliminated poachers from my list of possibilities. What now? Was this guy one of the people I met? None of the men spoke, so it was possible. But it seemed to me at the time that the woman was in charge. If so, she would have made the call. This guy was unfamiliar with me. I wasn't sure if it was the same group of people. But if not, who were they? And what did Michaela's mother have that they wanted?

"Do you have a plan?" asked Jon, breaking into my thoughts.

"I think I do, but it's going to be tight. We could use Joe's expertise. Do you think he'd want to come up—like soon?"

"Is that a serious question? Of course he would. I'll call him now and see if he can get up here by tomorrow."

Joe Gray was instrumental in the Wisdom Spring affair. A few months earlier, when I was missing in the wilderness, he dropped everything to help Jon and Jess find me.

Joe had unique skills honed by years as a CIA operative.

When he left the CIA, he became a private investigator, working primarily for the hotshot attorney Mill Colson. Known as the "Attorney to the Stars," Mill came to Jon and Jess's aid when Jess was accused of killing four coworkers. After the Wisdom Spring affair, Joe became Colson's head of security, but Joe also took on private jobs.

In this case, it was personal. And as much as Joe had helped us, we had also saved his life, so our connection with Joe—and his with us—was strong. Add Michaela's capture to the mix, and there would be no stopping him. I pitied anyone who got in his way. In his early fifties, Joe wasn't very tall and had no distinguishing features. He was the kind of person you could walk past and not even notice, which is probably why he was so successful in his job.

When Jon called, Joe said he'd take Mill's private jet from LA directly to Homer. He'd be there sometime in the morning.

While Jon was calling Joe, I called my friends at Piney Lake on a satellite phone. I explained the situation, stressing that the people who kidnapped Michaela might be Russians, based on the caller's accent and their interest in Michaela's mother, who, Michaela had told me, was Russian. They didn't need any more motivation than that, although the fact that Michaela was taken would have been enough, as they were quite fond of her, and loved her toughness—a quality they valued.

"There are four of us who can come down," said Ollie, the de facto leader of the community. "Will that be enough? We can bring lots of firepower."

"That would be appreciated," I answered.

"We'll be down in the morning."

Minutes after I hung up with Ollie, my phone rang. It was Special Agent Briggs calling from his burner phone. I almost didn't answer it, not wanting to involve the FBI, but then I figured that Briggs might have some important information.

He didn't. He was just checking in. Tell him about Michaela, or don't tell him? That was my dilemma.

He could tell that something was wrong.

"What are you not telling me?" he asked.

I kinda had to tell him now.

I explained about buzzing the woman and her friends in my plane.

"That was stupid," he said, stating the obvious.

"I know. But Michaela has been taken." I choked up as I said it.

"And you're just telling me this now? Are you crazy?"

"Sorry. There's too much happening all at once."

"Okay. Tell me about it."

"The people who took her sound Russian, whereas the woman who shot at Jon and me definitely seemed American. But they want me to meet them at the same place I had the run-in with the woman, so I don't know. The guy was clear that if I got the FBI involved, they would kill Michaela. I didn't want to leave you out of the loop, but at the same time, I couldn't take the chance of involving the FBI."

"I get it," he said. "So, what are your plans?"

I told him everything to date and about calling Joe and the Piney Lake gang.

"Sounds like you need another hand. I'm on vacation, so my presence wouldn't be official."

I was pretty sure he was lying to me about the "official" part. It seemed to me that even on vacation, he was still FBI. But he also wanted to help, and we could use as many hands as possible.

"I'll be down in the morning," he said.

The next morning was going to be busy, with Briggs, Joe,

and the Piney Lake crowd all showing up. That left me the rest of the evening to figure out what was happening.

Jon and Jess came over to help me go through the boxes. Of course, they managed to arrive at dinnertime.

"You two are something else," I said.

"Hey, do you think we're helping you go through the boxes without pay?" asked Jon.

I chuckled at his comment, but it was a hollow attempt at levity for both of us. Michaela was gone. It was as simple as that. Jess wasn't even trying to obscure the obvious. There was no question that she was taking this hard.

We ate a quiet dinner, each of us lost in our thoughts.

Finally, I said, "Enough of this. Michaela's gone, but she's not dead. I seriously doubt that these people—whoever they are—would harm a child. They want information and know that the only way they can get it is to force us to give it to them. This is how they're doing it. We need to go through the boxes tonight. Tomorrow's going to be a busy day. So, if there is something to find, we have to find it tonight."

"Then let's do it," said Jess. "How many boxes are there?"

"Probably about thirty of various sizes. I told the person on the phone they were in a storage locker. I planned to put them in a locker once Michaela was fully comfortable with the living situation. Right now, they're stacked in a spare closet."

We piled the dishes in the sink and transported all the boxes to the living room. If I was going to bring them all the boxes, I was going to go through them first. I had to find a clue to what all this was about. No way was I going into this blind.

We were able to eliminate some of the boxes immediately—those with clothes and pictures. Whatever we were looking for would be something she had probably hidden in papers or books.

We each took a box to go through. I think we all had the same thought that it was wrong to be doing this. These belonged to Michaela, not us. They were boxes that Michaela would eventually go through when the time was right. Not only were we invading her privacy, but the people who had her were expecting me to bring the boxes and lay bare to total strangers Michaela's mother's life.

Well, that wasn't going to happen.

I already knew her name—Natalya Orlova. Orlova was Michaela's last name before I adopted her. But I didn't know much more about Natalya. I knew she was about my age when she died and that she was beautiful. Michaela showed me a lot of pictures of Natalya. She died of stomach cancer—not a pretty way to go. She had married a guy named Sims, a thoroughly bad man who was thankfully no longer with us, and had Michaela. Natalya kicked Sims out of the house when she learned that he was having an affair—with someone who was also thankfully no longer with us. I had come to know both of them a few months earlier. Other than that, I knew nothing about Natalya.

My first box was full of books, mostly hardcover nonfiction on flowers and birds. I went through each book, looking for anything she might have hidden in the pages.

Nothing.

I put the box aside and moved on to the next one.

We were silent as we carefully sifted through every item in every box. It was hard because we had no idea what we were looking for.

I had just opened my fourth box when we had our first discovery.

"I think I found something!" said Jon excitedly.

He had his laptop open. A few minutes earlier, I had seen

him open it and insert a flash drive, but I was too involved in my box to pay much attention.

"I don't think Natalya was who Michaela thought she was."

"Not her mother?" I asked.

"No, not that."

"What was she?" asked Jess.

"I think she was a spy," said Jon.

He looked up from the computer.

"And not for our country."

Chapter 33

"A spy?" I asked.

"That's what it looks like," said Jon. "She made copies of messages she sent. I'm guessing she destroyed the originals. They are in Russian, but I'm copying and pasting them into the translation software. There's a communique from her from 2010 to some guy named Alexander at a trading company in Brussels."

"A trading company?" asked Jess.

"Yeah, aren't all spy networks under umbrella companies, and don't they all seem to be trading companies?" I asked.

"They are in the movies," replied Jon. "I'm not sure about real life, but this one seems to be. She tells Alexander that she found the munitions site, but it was empty."

"What munitions site?" asked Jess.

"That's it?" I asked.

"So far, but I'm still looking. But that sounds like spy stuff to me."

He stopped talking. I could tell that he'd found something.

"Definitely a spy," he said. "Here's another message. It was written about a month earlier than the first one. In it, she's tendering her resignation. She doesn't say KGB, but she uses terms like *Mother Russia*. Oh, and guess why she was retiring?"

"Easy," said Jess. "She was pregnant."

"You take the fun out of everything," said Jon, still flipping through the documents.

"It makes sense," replied Jess. "In 2010, she would have been pregnant with Michaela."

"Here's another one," said Jon. "It came after her resignation letter. This Alexander guy asks her to take on one last mission since she lives nearby. They need her to find an old munitions bunker in Alaska from the 1960s that was manned by a quasi-military group loyal to Russia. They lost contact with them, and no one ever followed up."

"I wonder why?" said Jess.

"If they were an independent group," I said, "the KGB could work with them but not be officially connected to them. Maybe they felt it would be too dangerous to enter U.S. territory to find them. And if the connection was ever made between the KGB and this group, it would result in a major situation between the two countries. Maybe it was felt that it would be better to cut their losses."

"So, putting them in order," said Jon, "she announces her resignation; then they ask her to look for this mysterious bunker; then she lets them know it was empty."

"Do you think she even went to look for it?" I asked.

Jon was silent. He had discovered something else.

"She found it," he announced. "She took pictures. Look."

We crowded around his laptop as he slowly scrolled through a dozen pictures.

"This look familiar?" he asked me.

"It looks a lot like the valley we landed in," I said. "But it's not. It's the second valley—the one closer to the shack I saw from the air."

"I think it is," said Jon. "Here's a picture of a wooden

shack."

"Probably the one I saw."

He flipped to a picture of the interior of the shack. Three skeletons lay on the floor. The next picture showed an open trap door. The picture after that was dark but showed at least a couple more skeletons. Another one showed a hallway. But again, it was dark.

"The scene at the bottom of the trap door?" suggested Jess.

"That would be my guess," said Jon.

"It looks like someone killed them," I said. "But who?"

"And if munitions were stored there, what happened to them?" asked Jon.

"And how much was there?" I added. "Are we talking about a small operation or something major? The shack isn't big enough to hold much, and what can they fit through that trapdoor?"

Finding information about the purpose of the shack and bunker was important. Michaela's mother's inability to find any trace of the munitions told me that they had already been moved out. But how many and where? At this point, it was probably anyone's guess.

But then, what if they were still there, and she just missed them? It would put Michaela in a perilous situation.

Those were all of the pictures on the flash drive.

But there was a second flash drive. Jon put it in the laptop and opened it.

There was only one document. With our heads almost touching, we read it.

"Oh ... my ... God!" said Jess.

We had only seen the tip of the iceberg!

Chapter 34

It was in English. It looked to have come from an American high military official, but the header was chopped off.

> ****TOP SECRET****
> ****FOR YOUR EYES ONLY****
> *June 22, 1966*
> *Be advised that the United States suffered a major theft of nuclear weapons last week.*
>
> *A Soviet fringe terrorist group is suspected to be behind it. Imperative that the weapons*
> > *are recovered before they fall into the hands of the arms dealer known as "The Russian." The magnitude of the theft has not yet been calculated, but it is known that several dozen M28 Davy Crockett Weapon Systems were stolen, as well as the corresponding M388 projectiles with the W54 nuclear warheads.*
>
> *If they get into the wrong hands, these weapons could wreak significant damage on cities*
> > *throughout the country.*

End of message.

"Is this saying what I think it's saying?" asked Jon.

"And if it is," I said, "how did Natalya get her hands on the message?"

"It must have been sent to her by this Alexander guy," I said.

"Do we know what these weapons are?" asked Jess.

"It's all Greek to me. I'll look it up now," I said.

"You mean you don't know this off the top of your head? What kind of men are you?" asked Jess.

"I've already threatened to drop Michaela from my plane. You're welcome to join her," I said.

"While you're looking up the weapon, I'll see if any public mention was made of the theft," said Jon.

The room was dead silent while Jon and I did our research. Jess opened her laptop and started typing.

About fifteen minutes later, Jon said, "Nothing about the theft anywhere. They must have wanted to keep this from the media."

"I can see why," I said. "These are nasty little things. The Davy Crockett Weapon System was a tripod with a launch tube and control switches. The tube was less than three feet long. The M388 projectile was almost as long as the tube and weighed about fifty pounds. But, what makes this fun is that the projectile has a nuclear warhead."

"Isn't that small for a nuclear bomb?" asked Jon. "Not that I know anything about nuclear bombs."

"What I'm reading says it was one of the smallest nuclear weapons ever built. They did away with them in the early '70s when it was determined that their short range could put our own troops in harm's way."

"Small or not," said Jess, "they are still nuclear. I know Natalya said they weren't there, but what if she was wrong? What if she missed them?"

"Then we have a whole shitload of nuclear weapons under Alaska," said Jon. "If they ever went off, it would change this country forever."

"And it means Michaela is right in the middle of it," I said. I was trying hard not to cry.

"While you guys were doing your research, I was doing some of my own," said Jess. "It mentions an arms dealer called 'The Russian.'"

"Yeah, I was going to come back to that," I said.

"Well, there isn't much about him. It seems he was quite an enigma. It was assumed he was Russian—hence the name. He was considered the most feared arms dealer in the world. Sometime in late 1966, he fell off the map. Totally. He was never seen or heard from again."

"It seems like 1966 was an eventful year," said Jon. "Did they ever find his records?"

"No. But it seems he had a son. The son took over the business and is known to be even better at it than his father. The son's nickname is The Ghost. No one has ever seen him, and no one knows who he is."

"The Russian? The Ghost? Not very original," said Jon.

"Despite that, it sounds like we have our hands full," I said.

*****

They all showed up the following day on three different

flights. The Piney Lake crowd certainly looked like survivalists. Three of the four had long beards, while only Ollie was somewhat clean-shaven. They were all dressed in jeans and flannel shirts.

The Piney Lake crowd already knew Joe but not Briggs. When I told them that Briggs was FBI, they weren't happy.

"I'm not here officially," said Briggs, immediately sensing their concern. "I'm here as a friend of Scott's. And you might like to know that when I transferred here, one of my first chores was to get up to date with any groups the FBI was watching. Although I ran across the name of your group, there was almost nothing in the file. They have no interest in investigating you."

That seemed to appease them marginally.

They were a rough crowd. As a bush pilot, they had accepted me a long time ago. Besides, they loved me when I let them dismantle a new helicopter that had been following us with some now-deceased bad guys. They cleared thousands of dollars on the parts. They had accepted Joe during the Wisdom Spring affair the minute he shot and killed one of the bad guys. In their eyes, Joe had immediately become one of them.

But Briggs knew he had to take it further to convince them of his trustworthiness.

"And you have my promise that I will quash any investigations about you that do pop up. Not that you have to worry—they won't."

From that point on, they were the best of friends.

We were all sitting in my living room, and I was telling them what Jon and I had discovered in the papers belonging to Michaela's mother.

"They have a shipment of Davy Crocketts?" asked Ollie.

"You've heard of them?" I asked.

"Sure. Dangerous weapons. They won't take out a whole city, but they'll do a lot of damage. Picture anywhere from ten to twenty tons of TNT. That's what the M388 projectile with the W54 warhead would be like."

"He can rattle it all off his head," Jess said to Jon and me. "How come you guys couldn't?"

"From 10,000 feet, you'd make a nice little splat on the ground," I answered.

She just gave me a mischievous smile.

I tried to stay calm, but the thought of Michaela up there with all of those warheads—if they were there—made me a little sick to my stomach.

"Why would they still want them after all this time?" asked Jess.

Joe answered that one.

"I don't know how many were stolen," he said. "Let's say it was fifty—or even just twenty-five. And that's just the weapon system itself. Who knows how many projectiles and warheads were stolen with them? It wouldn't mean anything to countries like Russia or China. We have so many regulations when it comes to the use of nuclear weapons; any large country would be stupid to use them. But what about a rogue country, or even worse, rogue factions within a country? If they have the means to purchase these weapons, think of the havoc they could wreak on a country. We've seen it so many times—the gangs in Haiti, the paramilitary groups in some African countries that destroy villages and kidnap the children. Even in this country, if the wrong groups get their hands on them, we're talking chaos."

"But would they still be good after all this time?" I asked.

"Depends," said Joe. "If they've been kept in ideal conditions, they would probably be just as potent. If conditions were less than ideal, they could be degraded. They could also leak radioactivity, which could be dangerous to anyone trying to handle them."

"Or in a room with them," added Ollie.

I immediately thought of Michaela.

"So, you think Michaela's mother might have been a Russian spy?" asked Joe, returning to business. "That would devastate Michaela if she found out."

"I don't know if she was," I said. "It seems so, but I don't know if there's any way to find out for sure."

"I'll find out," said Briggs.

He pulled a cheap phone from his pocket and hit speed dial.

"I only keep one number on this phone," he explained.

When the person answered, he said, "Hey, are you busy? You're what? You're out getting a bagel? Are you ever in the office?"

He got a response that made him laugh, then said, "Can you look up someone without setting off any alarms? Her name is Natalya Orlova. She's deceased, but I need to know if she was ever KGB. This is related to the other matter we discussed." He waited while the other person said something and replied, "Yeah, I know. I'm an idiot. But could you do it? A young girl's life hangs in the balance." The other person said something. "Yeah, I guess I should have said that in the beginning." More words on the other end. Then Briggs said, "Yes, you can still finish your bagel first. Thanks, Marty."

Briggs hung up, then said, "We'll know within the hour."

I made lunch for everyone. I tried to be as upbeat as possible, but it was hard. I was missing Michaela terribly. Jess, who was helping me, saw it on my face.

"We'll find her," she whispered to me.

I just nodded.

We were halfway through lunch when Briggs's phone rang. He listened for a minute, then said thank you and hung up.

"Yes, Natalya Orlova was a KGB agent for about ten years. She retired just shy of thirty, when she got pregnant."

"With Michaela," I said.

"Seems like it," he said. "It was about fourteen years ago."

"And Michaela is thirteen," I said. "That confirms it."

"She retired to Seattle, then moved to Anchorage. The CIA kept tabs on her for a while but finally determined that she was indeed retired. They never went after her or tried to kick her out of the country. They felt it would be better not to touch her, in case one of her former cohorts got in touch. From what my friend can determine, no one ever did."

"So what's our plan," asked Joe.

"They expect me to show up tomorrow morning with boxes of her stuff," I said. "They're probably most interested in her papers. A lot of the papers are in Russian, but not all of them are. The ones in English were worthless, but I have no idea about the Russian ones. All of the important stuff seems to be on the flash drive. Anyway, I'll fly up there and make the exchange—the papers for Michaela."

"They won't let you live," said Ollie.

"Of course they won't. That's why all of you are here. Later today, I'll fly you up by helicopter. If all the NTSB people are gone, I'll drop you off at *The Wonder Boys* plane crash site."

"They are gone," said Briggs. "The site is empty."

"It'll mean you guys will have to spend the night up there."

"I think we can deal with it," said Jon.

"In the early morning, you can all hike to the valley—I'll

give you directions. Briggs, you hiked the route from the plane to the crash site and back again, so it should seem familiar. Hopefully, you can fan out and wait for them. I'll draw a map and show you where I'll come in and taxi to. You can use that as your guide for where you can aim since that's where this group will meet me."

I suddenly realized what I was asking everyone to do.

"I have no idea what to expect. I don't know how many people they have or their intentions. I'm only assuming they are Russian by the caller's accent and because they want Michaela's mother's papers. But the woman Jon and I ran across wasn't Russian. I know there is a second valley where they probably have a plane, and not far from the second valley is an old building. I can only assume that they are using the building for something. I'm guessing that they haven't found the bombs and hope that Natalya knew something about it."

"So, are you bringing them all of Natalya's papers?" asked Jon.

"No," I said. "I have a better idea."

Chapter 35

A few hours after Michaela was shut in the room alone, the door suddenly opened, and one of the blonde men stuck his head in. He made a face. Michaela had peed in the bucket sometime earlier, and the room smelled sour.

The man pointed to the bucket and motioned for Michaela to follow him. As they climbed the ladder, Michaela held the bucket tight to avoid dropping it. A minute later, they were in the fresh air. It was chilly, but the air had never felt so good.

The man motioned for her to dump the bucket in the woods. Then, he gave her a cup of water to rinse the bucket. While she was rinsing it, she heard the men talking in Russian. They had decided that there was nothing in the "bunker," as they called it, and the Americans had already searched the surrounding area. So, they hoped that Michaela's mother's papers were a clue to what they were looking for.

What *were* they looking for?

The bald man told them to stay outside and be alert and said he would tell the girl that they'd all be in the building so she wouldn't be tempted to try an escape.

Could she escape that way? Even though it was only late afternoon, it was already dark. Maybe she could sneak out late at night.

The bald man told her what he told the others he'd say; then he had one of the blonde men lead her back to her room.

It was too early to try an escape outside. But knowing that no one would be in the building, Michaela decided to check out the bunker. Maybe she could find something she could use as a weapon.

Michaela waited half an hour, then slowly opened the door and peeked out. There was only dead quiet and darkness. She picked up her lantern and crept out into the hall. She already knew that the main room was to the right. So, she turned left.

The corridor continued for about fifty feet, then turned to the right. Along the corridor on both sides were doors. She opened each one as she passed and held the light inside the doorways. Most of the rooms were empty of anything that looked significant. But most had piles of junk. Maybe she could find a potential weapon among the junk. But she wanted to check out the other rooms first.

Some of the rooms had double sets of bunk beds. She counted sixteen beds in all. Another room was larger than the rest. It was a kitchen with a table and chairs for twelve people. This was once a busy place. But Michaela didn't think it had been used in many years.

It took her longer than she thought to investigate all the rooms. The corridor turned right again, and she eventually found herself back in the room with the trapdoor. So, the whole bunker was one rectangular hallway.

Michaela had to pee again, but the thought of the smelly bucket in her room disgusted her. And then it hit her.

The other rooms are old and smelly, she thought. *Why not just pee in a corner of one of them?*

Her best bet was to pick a room far from hers so the smell

wouldn't drift up to her room. And she knew the exact one. Carrying the lantern, she backtracked down the corridor parallel to hers until she reached the end. That room was the farthest from hers and was empty except for small piles of junk.

She entered the room and went to the far corner. After taking care of business, she was heading for the door when she tripped over something and fell.

"Ow," she exclaimed, shining the light toward whatever she tripped on. It was just a random piece of metal.

As Michaela stood up, she used the wall as support.

But wait. She felt something. The wall beneath her fingers had a crack in it. She held up the light. It was a long crack that ran from ceiling to floor, and it was almost impossible to see.

Maybe it was just how it was constructed, maybe all the walls had cracks, but her gut told her it was something else.

Michaela examined the walls with the lantern, but didn't see anything. Then she ran her hands along each wall and didn't feel the same crack. She went into the room next door and did the same thing. Nothing.

Michaela felt that everyone was looking for something and hadn't found it yet. Was this a clue? She went back into the first room and felt all around the wall. She pushed on the wall. It wasn't solid and seemed thinner than all the other walls.

The thin crack was about four feet from the corner, so Michaela went to the corner and ran her fingers up and down.

And that's where she found it—a latch. It was tiny and set back in the wall. It would have been almost impossible to find, even for someone looking for it.

She pressed the latch and heard a click. That section of the wall fell toward her.

It wasn't heavy, so she pulled it away and was presented with another door—a metal one set back about a foot. It had a lever for a handle.

Was it locked?

She pulled up on the lever. It moved easily, and the metal door opened. She pushed open the metal door, pulling the wall door behind her. It had a small metal handle that allowed her to pull the piece of wall back into place. The latch clicked, meaning the wall was again invisible from the other side. With the piece of wall in place, no one would know where she was.

Michaela held up the lantern and looked around. The room was massive—at least thirty feet in both directions.

And it was filled with weapons!

There were all kinds of weapons—machine guns, rocket launchers, and others she had never seen before—and stacks of boxes of ammunition. Was all this in preparation for an invasion of some kind?

At the back of the room was another door. Could it lead to the outside? She walked past the crates of weapons until she reached the door. Could this be her way to escape?

Michaela hesitated, then opened the door. It didn't lead to the outside but to another room. This room was larger than the first one and was piled high with wooden crates, but these crates were all sealed shut.

She held the light up to one of the crates. It had a symbol stenciled that she had seen before—maybe in the movies? It was yellow with black blade-looking things—the symbol for radioactivity!

She held the light to another box, then another. They all had the same symbol.

Then Michaela noticed that the crates on one side of the room were larger than those on the other. The larger boxes had the words M28 Davy Crockett, while the smaller boxes were labeled M388 Davy Crocket Projectile/W54 Nuclear Warhead.

Michaela had no idea what most of the words meant, but it didn't matter. She knew the word *nuclear*.

They had to be nuclear weapons.

This must be what the men were looking for!

Chapter 36

Was she in danger by being in the same room with nuclear weapons, if that's what they were? She didn't know, but she doubted it. She couldn't believe that they would be leaking radioactivity. The danger to her would be if they went off. But if they did, she would die instantly, so there was little she could do about it.

Was this why everyone was here? Were they looking for them? Was that what this was all about? If so, what did her mother have to do with it? Why would these men want to see her belongings?

The crates on one side of the room were long and rectangular. The other crates were roughly the same size, except they were square. She did a quick count. There were about thirty rectangular crates and even more of the square crates.

And then it hit her. There was no way they could have transported them through the trapdoor, so there had to be another entrance. Maybe she had a way out!

Shining the light, she saw a tunnel leading from the back of the room. Michaela started toward it, reached the entrance, and then stopped. She had been gone a while. Would they check on her? What would they do if they found her room empty? They would search for her, of course.

And then she laughed. It echoed down the tunnel.

If they couldn't find the munitions, they certainly wouldn't find her. Michaela made sure to close the wall and door behind her. To them, she will have mysteriously disappeared. They'd be out there scratching their heads. It was almost funny.

What wasn't funny was this room and everything stored in it. The boxes contained something radioactive. Bombs? She tried to remember what she knew about Davy Crockett. Not much. He was at the Alamo and was some sort of frontiersman. Putting together the little bit she knew about him with the names on the boxes, it made sense that these were weapons.

Michaela wished she had more than just a small lantern. There had to be a light switch somewhere. There. Right in front of her was a lever. Above it was a small sign written in Russian. It said "lights." She pushed it up. Nothing. Well, that made sense. When this place was being used, they probably had a generator to power the lights.

She looked down the dark tunnel. It seemed to go a long way. She needed a weapon, just in case an animal was waiting in the dark.

A weapon. Of course! Michaela turned around and headed back to the room that held the guns. She had seen handguns and rifles. Would they still work after all this time?

Michaela opened the door slowly, just in case her captors had discovered the room. No. It was quiet. She found the box of handguns. They were big, like Scott's .45. Kind of big for her, but if she had to, she could shoot it. Next to the guns were boxes of .45 ammunition and some empty magazines. How convenient.

She tested the slide on the gun. It worked. Making sure the gun was empty, she pulled the trigger. Nothing stuck, so she'd have to take a chance. She filled one of the magazines and put it in the gun; then she filled two more. Hey, if they wanted a war, she'd give it to them.

As she was leaving, Michaela saw an open box of machine guns. They looked like the ones she'd seen in a World War II movie. Nearby was ammunition and a pile of empty magazines.

What the hell, she thought. She filled up two magazines. Her fingers were getting tired of pushing the ammunition into the magazines, so she stopped after two. If that wasn't enough firepower, she'd never have enough. The machine gun had a strap, so she put the gun over her shoulder. She saw a box of hand grenades but decided against them.

They'd probably blow up in my hand, she thought.

Michaela was ready. She put the .45 in her belt and the extra magazines in her back pockets, then returned to the scary room with the nukes. She crossed the room and entered the tunnel.

She was right. The tunnel was long, and a set of train tracks ran down the center. A train? Then she saw what it was. Pushed off to the side was a flat car with wheels like a train.

"That's how they got the crates in here," she said quietly. Even softly, her voice echoed off the walls.

Michaela started walking. The tunnel sloped up slightly as she walked. After a half mile, the tunnel came to an end. She looked for a door and then realized that the whole end of the tunnel was a door. It was about the size of a garage door and looked thick. Using her light, she tried to find some kind of handle. Finally, she found one in the middle of the door.

And it was locked with a huge thick padlock!

All that work to get there, and she was in no better shape than before.

There was no way to escape!

Chapter 37

The call from the kidnappers came late that afternoon. I was prepared for it. I told the others about my plan, and they all agreed.

"Do you have the belongings of the girl's mother?" the Russian voice on the other end asked.

"I do," I said.

"And you'll bring them in your plane tomorrow morning?"

"No."

"No? Do you want to see your daughter dead?"

"No, I'm not bringing all her belongings because I don't need to. I looked through everything but found no papers. But what I did find was a flash drive. It contains everything I think you're looking for. It will save you from looking through her clothes, books, and memorabilia. It's all on the flash drive."

"Then bring the flash drive."

"Yes and no."

"What do you mean?"

"I transferred all the information onto another flash drive, one that is password protected, and I destroyed the original. Only I know the password to the new flash drive. I will only give you the flash drive and password when Michaela is safely in my arms. That's the deal—the only deal."

There was silence on the other end. Finally, the Russian agreed.

"This better not be a trick," he said.

"No trick. My only concern is for my daughter. I don't care about the other stuff. I'll be there around ten tomorrow morning. Is that acceptable?"

"Yes."

"Have Michaela where I can see her when I land."

"Okay."

*****

I loaded the Piney Lake crew, Briggs, Joe, Jon, and Jess, onto a helicopter soon after I got the call. It wasn't my helicopter, but I could use it whenever I wanted. Jess had made it clear that if I got all macho and told her that only the men should go, she'd slug me. I let her know that I hadn't planned on leaving her home. She was as much a part of the group as anyone. Besides, I didn't like to get slugged.

I had to make a decision about Max. There was no way I was leaving him out of this, but I had to decide if it would be better for him to come with me or go with the group. I finally decided that he would be more valuable with the group. I would be outnumbered when I arrived, and someone might choose to shoot Max.

Flying a helicopter at night wasn't my preference, but I had no choice. I knew where I was going and would only have to use the big lights to illuminate the landing spot when I arrived. I was pretty sure the people at the cabin wouldn't see the lights. Besides being two or three miles away, they were in the middle of the forest. I felt pretty safe that we wouldn't be seen or heard at that distance.

Between the people (and dog), the weapons, and the limited camping supplies, the helicopter was crowded. But somehow, we made it work. A couple of hours later, I made a somewhat smooth landing in the area the NTSB had cleared out.

I shook hands with everyone and thanked them for what they were doing. Jon and Jess got hugs. Max got a hug and a slobbery kiss. He might have been embarrassed in front of everyone, but I didn't care.

I went over the next morning's plan with them. Then, I waited while they set up tents on the edge of the landing zone before I left. They would leave their tents and backpacks there when they performed their mission, and I'd pick them up later in the helicopter. They wanted to be as unencumbered as possible when they made the trek to the valley where I would be landing.

On the way home, I thought about nothing but Michaela. If they had hurt her in any way, the violence I would inflict on them would be merciless.

Finally, as I approached Homer, I told myself that Michaela was okay and to think of positive things, like killing all who held her.

*****

It was a cold and murky morning when I took off in my Beaver. I hadn't slept well that night, but I was awake and ready to go after a long shower and three cups of coffee. I had set 10:00 as the meeting time to give everyone time to get into place. Knowing them, though, they had gotten up at dawn and been there for hours.

I flew in silence. When I flew alone, I often talked to myself or put some music on. Not this time. I was quiet because I was nervous. Michaela's life was at stake here, as were the lives of all who had chosen to help me. There was a lot on the line.

And then there was the issue of nuclear weapons. Seriously? How the hell did I get myself involved with nuclear weapons? All I could hope for was that the weapons had been found years ago and removed, and the reason they—or Michaela's mother—couldn't find them was because they weren't there. Best case scenario.

Actually, the best-case scenario was that I turned over the flash drive, and Michaela and I would leave.

The flash drive I was giving them only contained a portion of the contents of Natalya's flash drive. Did they really think I would give them everything Natalya had put in hers? I included a few items that looked official, including her note that she had found nothing. But I left out anything else I didn't want them to have, including the Top-Secret message from the U.S. military.

Now, if all went well, it really wouldn't matter because my crack team of operatives—led by Max, of course—might be able to eliminate our Russian friends.

My satellite phone rang. I carried that with me in case one of my strike team on the ground needed to contact me. It was Joe.

"Everything okay?" I asked.

"Not exactly," he said. "They are all going bonkers. We did a little investigating, found the cabin, and figured we'd follow them to where you're landing. But they're in panic mode. I speak a little Russian, so I'm getting the gist of the problem.

"Which is?"
"Michaela is missing."

Chapter 38

Missing? How could Michaela be missing? And if Joe's description was correct, it came as a surprise to her captors.

I told Joe that I would follow through with my end of the plan and figure out where to go from there.

I had to smile. Only Michaela could screw people up like that. Somehow, she gave them the slip. Was she somewhere out in the forest? Jon said he would send Max after her. He'd find her. I breathed a little sigh of relief. If they couldn't find her, they couldn't hurt her.

A little while later, I approached the makeshift runway. The valley was empty. I wasn't nervous now that I knew Michaela was missing, and because I knew my friends were in place.

As I lined up with the runway, I saw another plane coming in for a landing in the other valley three or four miles away.

Hmm. Interesting.

I landed the Beaver. Once again, the landing was bumpy, but the plane could handle it. I pulled up close to the faint trail leading into the woods toward the cabin. I waited in the plane until someone made an appearance.

Finally, a bald man emerged from the trees and waved to me. I got out of the plane, my hand on the butt of my gun in its holster.

"Mr. Harper. Good to see that you came alone."

"That was the plan."

"Of course."

"Where's Michaela?" I asked, knowing the answer.

"She is fine. She's back at the place we are using as our headquarters."

"Bring her here. This was supposed to be an easy hand-off. You give me Michaela, and I give you the flash drive."

"But how can we verify its authenticity?" asked the bald man. "We have a computer back at the camp. We can verify it there."

Until I knew where Michaela was, I didn't have much choice. I had to figure that Joe and the others were observing us, so I felt pretty safe. I followed the bald guy into the woods.

We were on a very old trail. Only faint remnants of it could be seen. Other than these guys and the woman and her gang, I don't think it had been used in a long time.

Speaking of the woman...

"When I came here before, there was a woman and three large men. Are they part of your group?"

He was quiet while he thought up an answer. Finally, he said, "No, those were others. They are not here now."

Meaning, of course, that they were now dead.

"Who do you represent?" I asked. "The KGB?"

"Let's just say that we are contractors."

"For the KGB?"

"The less you know, the better."

"I disagree, but I won't argue with you."

We walked in silence for a while before arriving at the cabin. Tents had been set up outside in what had once been a clearing. Now, it was just a mess of shrubs and roots.

Obviously, cleaning up the area hadn't been a priority. Four men with guns were waiting for us. Two of the men were blonde, and the two others were pretty nondescript.

"We're here," said the bald one. "Give me the flash drive."

"That wasn't the deal. Where's Michaela?"

He looked at the others. Their shoulders went up in a "we have no clue" sort of way.

"Let me guess," I said. "You've lost her."

"We have temporarily misplaced her," said the bald man.

"I thought so. Then I suggest you all put your guns on the ground."

I was taking a chance that my people were there. But it really wasn't much of a chance. I knew they were.

As I said it, the other four men all raised their guns. As they did, I heard guns cocking in the woods.

"You are surrounded," I said. "I suggest you don't try anything."

There's always one in every crowd. In this case, two. The two blonde men dropped their weapons, but the two nondescript men raised their pistols with the intent to shoot me. From the woods came four shots, and the two men went down.

Now, they were two nondescript dead men.

Jon, Jess, and Briggs entered the clearing with their weapons drawn. I noticed that the Piney Lake gang wasn't there. Neither was Joe. Smart. We needed some aces in the hole. The bald man just gave me a nasty look. I had thoroughly ruined his day.

Sadly, he wasn't the only one whose day was about to be ruined.

Chapter 39

Prescott's private plane soared over the Alaska wilderness.

"Are we close?" he asked the pilot.

"Yes, Mr. Prescott. According to the coordinates I was given, it'll just be a few more minutes. I'm about to begin my descent."

Next to Prescott was Hagen, and four heavily armed men were behind them.

"I don't know what to expect when we land," said Prescott, addressing the men, "so be ready for anything."

A minute later, he saw the valley where they would land. In the distance, he spotted another small plane that also appeared to be landing.

"I wonder where they're going?" he said.

"That looks like it might be a Beaver," said Hagen, "so it's probably a bush pilot bringing in some hunters."

"If they get in our way, we'll have to take care of them," said Prescott.

Prescott was entering uncharted territory, and he wasn't comfortable with it. He had always conducted business from the comfort of his home. And although he was in the arms business, he'd rarely had to order anyone killed. His father was different and had been directly responsible for the deaths of many people—competitors, those who had wronged him, and countless others. Prescott wasn't like his father. The arms he sold resulted in death, but he had never felt comfortable ordering the death of someone. So, to talk so easily about killing the hunters didn't sit well with him.

Nothing was sitting well with him. Much of his reputation as The Ghost had to do with image. People were afraid of him and trod gently when talking to him. His father had set the stage, and he had picked up from there. Prescott rarely had to meet a buyer or seller in person, which allowed him to maintain his fierce, almost mythical image. The less people knew about him, the better. He could threaten if he had to, but he never had to make good on the threats. The threat itself was enough to get the job done.

Sometimes, he felt like the Great and Powerful Oz—the man behind the curtain. All pomp and no circumstance. Well, he might finally have to get his hands dirty.

He checked his watch. His hand was shaking. Shit! Did Hagen see it? He glanced over. Hagen was looking out the window.

But Hagen had seen it. A little smile formed on his lips as he faced the window. He didn't know what to expect when they landed. Would Prescott live through the day? He hoped not. But either way, he had already set things in motion. If he survived, Prescott would arrive home to a very different situation.

The plane landed a few minutes later. There were already three planes at the end of the field. Prescott was dismayed. The information he had told his woman on the ground must have been correct. Others had found out about it. The bunker had remained a mystery for almost sixty years. But now it looked like a flea market parking lot.

"What do you think?" he asked Hagen.

"It looks like you were right. The secret is out."

Hagen knew that the various government covert organizations would send independent contractors, creating a chaotic situation. He sensed that a lot of people would die today. As long as Prescott was one of them, all of Hagen's work would have been worth it.

Yes, he could have picked up a gun and killed Prescott any time he wanted, but where was the drama in that? He wanted Prescott to suffer. If it weren't here, it would be when he got home and discovered what Hagen had done to his life. Sadly, by then, Hagen would probably be in so much pain, he wouldn't get to appreciate it. That's why he hoped that Prescott met his maker on this trip.

"Let's go," said Prescott.

The men exited the plane and headed in the direction Prescott assumed was correct. There was enough of a trail to indicate they were going in the right direction. It was a new trail, probably from all the groups arriving on the scene.

They walked for ten or fifteen minutes, with Hagen leading the way.

Suddenly, Hagen put up his fist. They all stopped.

Hagen heard voices from directly ahead of them. He gestured for them to leave the trail. They crept through the forest, the voices becoming louder.

Suddenly, there was an explosion.

Now the fun begins, thought Hagen.

*****

Prescott's pilot had turned the plane around in anticipation of Prescott's return. The other planes made him nervous, as did Prescott's words to his men. In addition, having four heavily armed men in the back of the aircraft didn't sit well with him. He was a pilot, and that's all he was. He knew Prescott's occupation but never had to get involved in any of it. Prescott paid him well, but well enough for this? His job was to shuttle the man back and forth to meetings with his banker on the Cayman Islands and to take Mr. Hagen to his meetings with arms dealers. Despite the purpose of the meetings, there was never any danger. This was different. Somehow, he felt that this wasn't going to end well.

Usually, when he was waiting, he would read a book. Not this time. He was on alert for anything that seemed "wrong." A half-hour later, he heard it.

In the distance, he heard an explosion. Then he heard gunshots—a lot of them. The gunfire didn't last long, but it was intense. A war was going on.

That was enough for him.

"Screw Prescott, Hagen, and all the rest," he said to the empty cabin. "I don't get paid well enough for this."

He decided he'd fly to Anchorage, leave the plane there, and take a commercial flight to somewhere Prescott would never find him—assuming Prescott even lived through it.

He taxied down the field and was in the air in seconds.

It was time to disappear.

Chapter 40

We were all standing in the middle of the clearing with the bald guy and his two blonde henchmen when I heard a rifle cock from the other side of the woods.

"How about you all put your weapons down?"

What now? I thought.

Nobody moved.

"Seriously, we could kill you all now, but we don't want to." His voice had a slight accent.

Slowly, we all set down our weapons, and three men stepped out from the woods. They had a vague Middle Eastern look about them.

"Now, who will tell us where the munitions are?"

"And who are you?" asked the bald man.

"An interested party."

"Mossad?"

In his mind, the bald guy must have thought he was still in charge. Frankly, I didn't know who was in charge. And it was about to get murkier.

From a different section of the woods came another voice. This one sounded American.

"Let's all set down your guns."

Five more men emerged from the trees. Were the trees

breeding them?

The three men who were momentarily in control set down their weapons. Their reign hadn't lasted long.

"It seems we've all come for the same thing," said the American. "Who's going to tell me where it is?"

"No one," I said, "because what you are all looking for doesn't exist."

"What do you mean?"

"A Russian spy thoroughly investigated this place in 2010 and determined that the weapons you are looking for weren't here. I have her finding on a flash drive that I was going to give these guys for the return of my daughter, who they kidnapped. I'm only here to get my daughter. The rest of you are shit out of luck. I don't know what happened to the weapons—the M28 Davy Crockett Weapon System, right?"

The American nodded.

"Someone got to it a long time ago."

"You're sure of that?"

"Well, let's look at the history here. The weapons were stolen from the military in 1966. In 2010, a Russian spy was sent here to find the weapons. What she found instead were a few skeletons and no weapons."

"The skeletons are still here," said the bald man.

"You didn't even clean them up?" I said. "What terrible housekeepers."

I was trying to sound confident, but I was anything but confident.

How did they all find out about this, and all seemingly at the same time? Someone must have informed them. But why? To create havoc? More likely, money was involved—a lot of it. Someone knew about this place and what it held, and decided it was time to make some money on that knowledge.

The other question was how they all managed to be here without seeing each other. They all had to fly in. Was it a case of the second plane to arrive saw that they weren't alone? Then, the third plane saw that two other groups had beaten them to it. I looked up at the overhanging trees. Seeing another plane come in would be hard for anyone on the ground. And we were far enough away from the second valley to hear a plane land. So, it was possible that the first group didn't know about the second, and the second didn't know about the third.

Was it a coincidence that they all arrived almost simultaneously? Or did they all find out at the same time and immediately act on it? I was never a big believer in coincidence, so the second explanation seemed the most logical.

It also told me how valuable these weapons were.

"I'm just trying to get a handle on this," I said. "I assume you are all independent contractors working for different organizations. You," I said, pointing at the bald guy, "are KGB. You three," I pointed to the second group, "are most likely Mossad. Our newest friends reek of CIA. There was another group here, led by a woman. I don't know who they were."

"They worked for an arms dealer," said the bald guy.

"Let me guess," I said, "someone who calls himself The Ghost? The son of a man with an equally exciting name called The Russian, who disappeared around the same time as all of this? Maybe one of your skeletons belongs to him."

No one said anything. So, I continued.

"How are we going to solve this? An FBI agent from Anchorage named Briggs knows exactly where I am. A CIA agent named Joe Gray also knows where I am."

Joe still hadn't shown himself, but Briggs gave me a look.

"We have the KGB, Mossad, and CIA all represented here. And they couldn't even do it themselves. They had to send contractors so they could claim deniability. And you're all here for nothing. The thing you're looking for doesn't exist. My suggestion? You all go home."

Out of the corner of my eye, I saw a streak of gray in the woods. The one-dog cavalry had arrived from somewhere. Had he been looking for Michaela?

"You know we can't do that," said the American. "I think the munitions are still here, and we'll be long gone with them before your FBI and CIA friends arrive. And since you guessed correctly that we are contractors for the CIA, having the CIA here won't be a problem for us."

Ollie and his three friends stepped out of the woods.

"Yes, you have a problem. I've listened to you, and you all make me sick," said Ollie.

Jon, Jess, Briggs, and I all picked up our weapons. But then, so did the KGB and Mossad people.

I looked around and said, "Not counting the two dead men, I count about twenty of us, all with guns pointed at someone else. I believe they refer to this as a Mexican standoff."

I was scared. This could turn bloody very quickly. If one person pulled the trigger, we all would, and I don't know who would be standing in the end.

And then an object was thrown from the woods. It bounced once and came to rest near the three groups across the clearing.

It was a hand grenade!

Chapter 41

When Jon and the others first arrived on the scene before Scott landed, Max went off alone—a dog with a mission. He sensed Michaela's disappearance and instinctively knew that was why Scott and the others had come here.

He could sense Michaela not far away and knew she was in trouble. It wasn't that he could smell her, although as he skirted the cabin and open area in front, he smelled that she had been there. He ran across the pee that she dumped in the woods.

Yes, he could smell her scent, but that wasn't what drove him. Max and Michaela had a connection that formed the first time they met. They had bonded at the soul level. Max wasn't relying on Michaela's scent. He was relying on something much deeper. And because of it, he found himself going in the opposite direction of the cabin. Michaela wasn't in the cabin. She wasn't even under the cabin. She was someplace else.

As he made his way through the woods, Max heard people walking. Humans were so noisy. He hid behind a tree and saw three men walk by. They all had guns in holsters. Max was intimately familiar with firearms. His police training had been extensive.

He immediately felt the aura of negativity surrounding them.

They passed by. Max could help Scott and the others, but he had a mission. Finding Michaela was first and foremost in his mind.

He kept going.

Another group of loud humans. Would they ever learn to move quietly?

A group of five. More negativity. More guns. He watched them pass.

He came around a tree. A bear was snuffling around, looking for something to eat. He saw Max and stopped. They stared at each other.

Then Max snarled. The bear stood, showing his claws. Max snarled again, his intent obvious. *Get out of my way, bear.*

The bear sensed a drive from Max, one he didn't want to get in the way of. He moved away slowly, then disappeared into the underbrush.

Max knew he had to get back to help Scott's friends, but he couldn't. Not until he found Michaela.

Max was heading in a line away from the cabin. He stayed on that path because it's where he felt Michaela. Now, he felt her presence below him.

He came across a low hill. It was a rock formation, but it wasn't. Something about it didn't feel natural. He sniffed around the base of the rocks.

It was here. This was where he would meet Michaela.

He sat by a rock and waited.

Chapter 42

A padlock.

All the work Michaela had done to get to this point, and she gets stopped by a padlock. And this wasn't some cheap hardware store lock. This one meant business. It was a foot long, made of heavy-duty steel.

But she had to try to break it. She looked in the rail car on the tracks near the door. Nothing. Then she walked back down the tunnel until she reached the overturned rail car. There, a steel bar. She picked it up. It was heavy, but she could carry it. If this couldn't break the lock, nothing could.

Michaela was exhausted when she arrived back at the door with the padlock. She sat on the ground and rested.

Was Scott looking for her? Did he even know where she was? He had to. She heard the bald man instructing him to collect her mother's belongings. Scott would call Jon and Jess, Joe, and Special Agent Briggs. Would he call Ollie and his gang? Maybe.

It didn't really matter. If she couldn't escape, Scott could do nothing for her.

She wished Max was with her. Max always calmed her down. He had a steady presence. It was almost like he knew what she was thinking.

Okay, enough wasting time. It was time to break the lock.

Michaela put the metal bar between the lock's U-shaped bars. She thought she remembered Scott calling it a shackle. She tugged on the bar. Nothing. She rearranged the bar, using a piece of the rock as a fulcrum, and pulled again—still nothing.

She adjusted it again and this time tried pushing on the bar. It slipped out of the lock, and Michaela flew into the door.

She cried out in pain and rubbed a bruised shoulder. She also hit her head. Touching it, she felt blood. It was only a scratch, but it hurt.

This wasn't going to work.

She sat back against the rock and surveyed the scene. There had to be a way out. Tears welled up in her eyes. No! She wasn't going to cry. She had to think.

And then it came to her. It would be dangerous. It could kill her. Even if it didn't kill her, it might alert the others to her location. Well, she didn't have much of a choice. She looked at the metal car on the tracks. It was heavy, and it was rusted in place. It wasn't going anywhere. Could it provide enough protection?

There was only one way to find out.

Michaela set down the metal bar and walked back down the tunnel. It was a long walk, but she had no other options.

Finally, she reached the area with the nukes. All was quiet. She tiptoed past the crates of nuclear weapons. She wasn't sure why she was tiptoeing, but it seemed like the thing to do.

She reached the door to the room with the other weapons and opened it in increments, half expecting the bald man to jump out at her. But all was quiet.

Michaela knew where she was going. She walked to the box that held the hand grenades and picked up three of them. Hopefully, she would only need one, but if it didn't work, she couldn't return for more.

She held them carefully as she left the room, closed the door behind her, and crept through the scary room. Once she was in the tunnel, she felt a little better.

Was this a stupid idea? Yeah, it was. She knew nothing about hand grenades besides what she had seen in movies. For it to blow up, she needed to pull the pin. In the movies, it always took a few seconds to blow. Did she have enough time to hide?

She was beginning to have second thoughts. What if she pulled the pin, and it went off immediately? Well, she wouldn't have anything to worry about ever again, would she? Could it set off the nuclear devices in the room down the tunnel? Probably not. At least, she hoped not.

Michaela put the two hand grenades on the ground and sat next to the door. Could she do this?

Enough! Just do it.

Michaela stood up and walked down the tunnel, hiding two hand grenades around a bend and behind a pile of rocks. If she needed another one, it should be far enough away from the explosion.

She walked back to the lock and positioned the grenade in the middle of the shackle, with the pin and handle of the grenade facing out. Michaela looked down at her hand and realized that she was shaking.

Stop! I can do this, she thought.

She looked back at the train car. The metal sides should protect her ... hopefully.

Here goes nothing.

Putting her left hand against the grenade to stabilize it, she pulled the pin with her right. As she did, the handle flew off.

A chill went through her body. Was that supposed to

happen?

She ran back and dove behind the car. The explosion came a second later. It was loud in the confined space, but not as loud as she thought it would be. Dirt and rocks showered her. She looked around the corner of the train. All she saw was dust.

Had her captors heard it? She didn't think so. Maybe its age had made it less powerful. Well, if it did the job, that was all that mattered.

The dust had cleared to the point that she could see the lock. What lock? It was gone. The explosion was successful! Interestingly enough, the door itself was unharmed. While that meant it was a solid door and probably very thick, it also might be hard for someone her size to open. Well, she'd deal with that in a few minutes.

Michaela went back and picked up the other two grenades. Now that she knew how they worked, she wasn't afraid of them. She put them in her jacket pockets and picked up her .45 and machine gun. She felt like a one-person army.

She inspected the door. It looked like it opened outward and up, so she pushed on it. Now, she'd find out if it was all worth it. She pushed. It was heavy, but it moved ever so slightly. Michaela stopped and rested. All she needed to do was move it enough to squeeze under it.

Michaela pushed again. It moved a little more. Fresh air blew in the space. She was almost free. One more push and the opening would be large enough to fit under. She took off her jacket and pushed the machine gun, pistol, and jacket with the grenades under the door; then she crawled through.

She was free!

Michaela looked up, and her mouth dropped open.

Sitting outside and waiting for her was Max.

Chapter 43

Michaela couldn't believe it. How in the world…?

"Max!"

Max ran and nuzzled up against her. She hugged and kissed him. And then she started to cry. Everything she'd gone through over the last two days rushed to the surface. She held onto Max with all her strength. Max seemed to understand what was happening and let her squeeze the stuffing out of him. He licked the tears off her face, only succeeding in making her face wetter than it had been with the tears.

Eventually, Michaela let go. She had made it out alive! And she couldn't ask for a fiercer protector than Max.

"How did you know where I was?"

Not getting an answer, she hugged him again.

"Where's Scott?"

Max gave a soft "woof" and turned, heading for the trees.

"Wait for me," said Michaela, gathering her pistol and machine gun and putting on her jacket with hand grenades in the pockets. She looked at the door. Whoever had built the tunnels had made the door blend in with the ground. She could have walked right on top of it and not seen it. Should she try to push the door closed or leave it open? Max was already in the trees, which helped her decide to leave it as it was.

Max wasn't stopping. He moved through the underbrush just slowly enough for Michaela to keep up.

The machine gun wasn't light—at least for a 13-year-old—so she couldn't run as fast as she wanted.

She was falling behind Max.

"Hey, wait up."

She almost expected him to respond, but instead, he slowed down. He seemed anxious to find Scott. Michaela hoped everything was okay.

Fifteen minutes later, she heard voices. Max had disappeared, but she wasn't worried about him. Max knew his job.

Michaela slowed down. She heard Scott talking. She dropped to her knees, crawled behind bushes, and observed the scene.

And what a scene it was.

Scott, Jon, Jess, and Special Agent Briggs were there. She saw Ollie and three others from Piney Lake. Scott really had called out the cavalry!

Facing them were what appeared to be three separate groups. Her captors were in one group—now with two of them dead on the ground—and eight others made up the other two groups. And everyone was pointing a gun. Scott and the others had their weapons pointed generally toward all the groups. The others didn't seem to be sure exactly who to aim at.

Michaela was an action movie buff. She had seen enough of them to know what could happen here. There were a lot of guns. One flinch, one accidental pull of the trigger, and one wrong move could turn into a bloodbath. And Scott would be in the middle of it.

She had to do something—and fast. She had to distract them.

And then she remembered the hand grenades. She pulled one out of her pocket. Hey, she was an expert with them now. There was no time to waste. Michaela pulled the pin and tossed it underhand into the middle of the clearing, farther away from Scott and his group and closer to the others.

Panic ensued, and the three groups dove for cover. Scott and the others just backed up into the trees.

The grenade exploded, sending up a cloud of rocks, plants, and dirt.

Michaela dove for cover as a barrage of gunfire erupted from the clearing.

Then, as quickly as it had begun, it stopped.

Chapter 44

The grenade exploded, and I was immediately covered in dirt.

We had taken cover in the trees, but the other groups weren't so lucky. They were too far out in the open to escape the blast. When the smoke cleared, three men were down, and the others were getting to their feet, some looking around for their weapons.

Ollie and his group began shooting, but the volley lasted only a few seconds. Three more men were down, and the rest raised their arms in surrender.

Briggs addressed the ragged remaining members of the groups.

"I'm Special Agent Duane Briggs of the FBI. I don't care who you are all working for; you're all under arrest."

Duane. So, he did have a first name. He didn't look like a Duane, though. I wasn't sure what a Duane was supposed to look like, but not that.

I'm not sure the people he addressed were in good shape.

They would be in even worse shape a minute later.

"Scott?"

It was Michaela's voice from the woods. I knew it! She had thrown the hand grenade. Only Michaela would do something like that. But her voice sounded funny. Something was wrong.

"Michaela?"

Max appeared next to me, ready for action. I held his collar. I had a bad feeling and didn't want Max to get caught in the middle of anything.

A man emerged from the trees with his arm around Michaela's neck.

"Who does this girl belong to?" he called out. He was an older man—maybe in his seventies—with dyed black hair. For his age, he looked to be in great shape.

"Me," I said, stepping into the clearing. "But don't hurt her."

"I have no intention of doing so."

He nodded toward the ragged group across the clearing from us, and suddenly, a hail of bullets came from near him and cut down the remaining contractors.

The shooting stopped as quickly as it had begun. It was bloody, violent, and enough to make a person sick. Yes, just a few moments earlier, we had been in a gunfight with the same group, but they were shooting at us, so it was a case of self-defense.

This was different. Their weapons had been set down on the ground, and their hands were in the air. This was a massacre, and the man who initiated it was nothing less than a monster.

And now he had Michaela!

I would have to tread carefully if I wanted any of us to survive this. Briggs was next to me, but the rest were hidden in the trees.

"I'm her father," I said. "What do you want?"

"You know what I want. I want the munitions."

"As I explained to the others, there are no munitions. The place is empty."

"Then there is no reason to keep the girl alive, is there?"

"Yes, because she is only a girl."

"If there are no more munitions, how did the girl come across a vintage machine gun, an old .45, and a hand grenade? She didn't bring them with her, so she clearly found them here."

I was confused, so I looked at Michaela and raised my eyebrows.

"I found them, Scott. I'll take him to them because he'll never find them on his own. But if he hurts you or any of the others, I won't tell him."

"What makes you think that I won't find them on my own?" asked the man.

"Because many people have spent a long time looking and haven't found them," I said.

"You won't find them on your own," said Michaela. "Trust me, you need me."

"So, do we have a deal?" I asked. "You don't harm anyone in our group, and Michaela will take you to the munitions—providing that I come too."

"We have a deal. Have your people come out and lay down their weapons."

Jon, Jess, Briggs, and Ollie and his boys all stepped out from the trees. Joe still wasn't with them. Joe hadn't shown himself earlier, so there was no reason for them to know he existed.

Five men emerged from the trees behind the man.

"Do you have a name?" I asked.

"I believe I have been referred to as The Ghost. The man next to me is named Hagen. You don't need to know the names of the others. I will leave two men to guard your people. Two of my men and Mr. Hagen will accompany us to the munitions.

Try to trick us, and the girl dies."

Why did everyone feel they had to say, "the girl dies?" Was there something about Michaela that brought it out in them?

I looked over at the others. They were on their knees, with their hands on their heads. I wasn't worried about them. I knew that Joe was right there. Joe would take care of the guards when we were out of sight. I knew that he usually carried a silencer with him. He was probably screwing it on right now.

Luckily, Jess had sent Max into the woods. He was probably with Joe right now.

"Let's go," said The Ghost.

The Ghost. Stupid name, if you asked me.

Michaela led us into the building. We passed three skeletons—two of them were near the door. The Ghost stared at them as we passed. He stopped, reached down, and picked up a tattered bag on a rusted chain. He grunted, dropped it, and then told Michaela to keep going.

She led us to a trapdoor with a ladder.

"We have to go down here," she said. "Just because we'll be underground, doesn't mean you'll know where they are. You still need me to find them. Nobody else has been able to."

Insurance to make sure they didn't think they were already there.

At Michaela's direction, we grabbed lanterns and climbed down the ladder. The Ghost's man, Hagen, was the first down, followed by his other two men, me, Michaela, and then The Ghost himself. I saw two more skeletons.

This place would make one heck of a Halloween haunted house.

We started down the dark hallway. Michaela pointed to the

first room on the left.

"This is where they kept me after kidnapping me," she said. "The bald guy was in charge."

If he wasn't already dead, I would have killed him.

"I was down here by myself," continued Michaela. "It's why I was able to find the guns."

"Were there big crates, too?" asked The Ghost.

He was looking for the Davy Crocketts.

"Yes."

We kept walking down the dark hallway. I glanced in each of the rooms as we passed.

Michaela had to endure being down here by herself? My admiration for her grew every day, not that it could really go any higher.

But it was time to focus on the current situation. The minute Michaela showed them the door to the weapons room, they were going to kill us.

"So your father was the one known as The Russian?" I asked The Ghost. "Was he one of the skeletons at the top of the stairs?"

"Yes to both of your questions. And don't ask me any others."

Okay, that didn't go well.

Michaela was walking next to me and nudged me. I looked over at her, and she motioned with her eyes to look down at her left hand, which was next to me and partly out of her jacket pocket. In her hand was a grenade.

She never ceased to amaze me.

Michaela slipped it into my right hand. With the darkness in the hallway, no one saw the handoff. Now, I just had to figure out when to use it.

We turned a corner.

"Is it much farther?" asked The Ghost.

"Nope," answered Michaela.

In a minute, we reached the last room of that hallway.

"It's in here," said Michaela.

We turned into the room, and Michaela went to the corner and flipped a switch. A part of the wall came away.

"How did you find this?" asked The Ghost.

I think he was as impressed by Michaela as I was.

"By accident," she answered.

"I'm almost sorry you'll have to die," he said, motioning to one of his men.

The man lifted his rifle, and as he did, I pulled the pin on the grenade and stuck it in the man's coat pocket. Then I gave him a push, grabbed Michaela's hand, and ran out the door. We turned right and dove to the floor of the hallway. From the room came a muffled explosion. Dirt, dust, and a piece of an arm flew out of the doorway.

I immediately scrambled up.

"Are you okay?" I asked Michaela.

Considering I had landed on top of her, I was more worried about crushing her than I was that she had been hit by shrapnel.

"You could lose some weight," she said, struggling to stand up.

She was fine.

I looked into the room. The Ghost's two henchmen were most obviously dead. The one with the grenade in his pocket had collided with the other one when I pushed him, and they had landed on top of each other. It was a gruesome scene.

On the other hand, The Ghost was still alive and struggling to stand up. He had lost his weapon someplace. I wasn't worried about him. The one who worried me was Hagen, his right-hand man. Hagen had opened up a second door and was already through it.

Hagen looked at me and said, "His name is Prescott. He lives on Long Island in the guise of a philanthropic businessman. But he's not. Besides being an arms dealer, he's a sad excuse for a human being. I'm sorry you have to be here."

"What do you mean?" I asked as he was closing the door behind him.

"I'm sorry you are all going to die."

He slammed the door.

Chapter 45

"Hagen! What the hell? What are you doing?" yelled The Ghost—who I now knew as Prescott.

"You deserve to die with the others," yelled Hagen from behind the door. It was a metal door, but not very thick. I could hear him, although he sounded far away.

"Actually," Hagen continued, "the others shouldn't have to die. Just you. Sadly, they will be collateral damage."

"I don't understand," yelled Prescott through the door.

"I've hated you for years. I've been trying to figure out how to kill you, and I finally know. I'm dying. I have cancer. But I may as well go out with a bang and take you with me. Oh, and not that it matters now, but in case I wasn't able to kill you, I've been funneling money out of your accounts into accounts under my name. You gave me just a little too much responsibility for your vast fortune, and I've taken advantage of it. Since I'm going to die, there will be no way to reclaim that money. Simply stated, you're broke. Goodbye, Prescott."

Prescott was stunned.

"You can't trust anyone," he said quietly. "It was a mistake to give him so much latitude. I don't usually make mistakes, but I made a big one with Hagen."

I wasn't sure if he was talking to me or himself. Regardless,

I didn't need to hear the self-reflection right now.

"Can he do that?" I asked, breaking into his *Oh, woe is me* moment. "Can he set off one of the bombs?"

"He was an EOD man in the Army. Yes, I believe he can."

There was a sudden change in Prescott. A few minutes earlier, he was a man in charge. A man used to getting his way without regard to how he got it. Now, he just seemed lost. Was it the betrayal of his right-hand man? More likely, it was the loss of money. I didn't know a whole lot about arms dealers, but my guess was that to be successful, you had to have a lot of money. Prescott had none now. He struck me as someone who had always gotten his way. You did what he said with no questions asked. Power was what he was all about. All of a sudden, he had power over nothing. But someone like him probably had the connections to reverse everything Hagen had done. It didn't matter. If I had my way, he wasn't leaving here alive.

Hopefully, the rest of us would.

"Let's go," I said. "We should get out of here."

I pushed Prescott ahead of us as we quickly made our way through the tunnels to the ladder leading up through the trapdoor.

One by one, we reached the top of the ladder. Once we were all assembled outside, we discovered Prescott's remaining men on their knees with their hands on their heads. They were being covered by one of Ollie's men.

It turned out that when the hand grenade went off down below, Prescott's men were distracted. Overpowering them was easy work for Ollie's guys.

I quickly explained what happened.

"So, this man Hagen—a dying man with nothing to lose— is alone underground with a shipment of nukes?" asked Briggs.

"This is way above my pay grade. I've got to call it in."

"How long would it take for reinforcements to arrive?" asked Jon.

Briggs frowned. "Too long."

"Then we need to get in there and stop him," said Ollie. "Do you know what it would do to the Alaska landscape if even one of those things went off? I live in this state. I don't want to lose it."

"They are small nuclear warheads," I said. "Will one do that much damage?"

"Underground and by itself, it could do a lot of damage, or the worst of it could be contained by the rock," said Ollie. "It's hard to say. The problem is that these are old nukes without all the safety mechanisms that the new ones have to prevent one from triggering another. They are all in a confined space, so it's possible that one could set off all the others. If that happens, we're talking major devastation."

"We have to do something," said Jess.

"You said that the message read that there were a lot of Davy Crocketts stolen," said Ollie.

"There were a lot of crates," said Michaela.

"Then they couldn't have brought them in through the trapdoor. There has to be another entrance."

"There is," said Michaela. "It's about a half mile from here. I can show you, but we'll have to run. They are in a different room. He has to go through one room to get to it. All the nukes are in the second room, but they're all boxed up."

It was weird how easily the word "nukes" came off her lips. She was growing up way too fast.

"Do we have time?" I asked.

"We might," said Ollie. "It just depends on how good and how fast he is."

"Okay, Michaela," I said. "Show us where it is."

I debated getting her to the plane and flying out of there to get her to safety, but I couldn't do that. It would be signing the death sentence for all the others. Michaela was one of us now. She'd either survive with us or die with us. And I knew she wouldn't want it any other way.

Then I had to think about Prescott. He was an evil man—one I could trust no further than I could throw him. He was indirectly responsible for countless deaths. Not to mention all the CIA, Mossad, and KGB independent contractors he had just killed.

But I wanted him with us. Hagen's hatred for Prescott seemed intense, so Prescott wouldn't be able to talk any sense into him. But maybe he could give us some insights into Hagen that would give us a psychological advantage. As for talking sense into him, I'd have to try to do that myself.

I'd also have to watch Prescott carefully. He got to where he was by being more intelligent and cunning than anyone else. He might be broke, but that didn't mean he was done. If we were successful in stopping Hagen, the first thing he was going to do was try to escape, and he wouldn't care who he killed in the process.

It was decided that Briggs, Joe, and Ollie would join us—Joe because of his history in covert operations, Briggs as a current FBI agent who could document and verify what we found, and Ollie because he was itching to be involved. He also seemed to have a working knowledge of bombs, which might come in handy.

Assuming, of course, we didn't get blown up.

Ollie's friends volunteered to watch Prescott's men. That left Jon and Jess. They were going to check the skeletons in the building to try to figure out who they were. They'd be doing it all the while not knowing if they were about to be blown up.

We took off through the trees, Michaela and Max leading the way. Max seemed to know exactly where to go. That was puzzling. I was going to have to ask Michaela about that.

Prescott had been quiet. What was going through his mind? Was he reevaluating his life? Yeah, right. People like him don't go in for self-evaluation. He was probably trying to figure out how to get out of this mess, and then where to get the money to keep his very profitable business afloat. With a reputation like his, I couldn't imagine it would be that hard. That meant he was plotting, and I needed to divert his thinking.

"So," I said as we tried to keep up with Michaela and Max, "tell me something."

"What?" he said.

"Tell me about *The Wonder Boys*, and why they had to die."

Chapter 46

"It was the result of a major screw-up. They shouldn't have been involved at all. The sad part was that, as a teenager, I loved their music. I was sad when they died."

"You knew they were dead?" I asked.

"It was the logical conclusion. My father lost contact with his man, so it wasn't hard to put two and two together."

"So, what happened?"

"An operative carrying a briefcase filled with a million dollars was about to be caught by the Feds. It was half of what my father was paying for the arms. There's supposedly a big supply of weapons here, but only the shipment of Davy Crocketts interested him. He already had a few potential buyers—including an African nation planning to take over another one. For something like that, these weapons were perfect. One blast could destroy everything within a hundred or more meters. What better way to take over a small country?"

As he talked, we jogged and walked between trees, rocks, and streams, with Michaela and Max leading the way. I wasn't sure how much I'd get out of him—it was already more than I expected. He seemed deflated.

"*The Wonder Boys* had just finished a concert and were loading equipment into a truck just as the operative passed. To avoid getting caught, he put the suitcase in an open box. Long story short, another operative tried to retrieve the suitcase but could not."

"Was his name Travis Miller?" asked Briggs. We all stayed together, with Michaela and Max slightly ahead of us.

"That was the name he went by in America, but it wasn't his real name. I have no idea what it was. My father arranged the flight to Fairbanks using two of our own pilots. But it was never going to go to Fairbanks. The plan was for them to go directly to the bunker. Something must have happened on the flight."

"Since you've given us this much background," I said, "I guess I can tell you that a CIA agent boarded the plane at the last minute. We know that there was a gunfight on board because we found the shell casings. That must have led to the crash."

"Did the NTSB find the suitcase?" asked Ollie.

There was no question about what he was thinking.

"Not that anyone reported," said Briggs.

I could see the wheels turning in Ollie's head. It just added incentive to stop Hagen from implementing his plan.

"We're here," said Michaela.

I looked at the slightly open door. It resembled a garage door but had been painted gray to look like the rock around it. Small rocks had been glued on it to complete the picture. A lot of effort had gone into concealing the bunker.

"Do you know what this was originally used for?" I asked Prescott. He was out of breath. He looked in good shape for his age, but it still couldn't have been easy going over the rough terrain.

"Some idiotic plan by a Soviet fringe group to take over America. They had other bunkers, too. They contacted my father about the arms after they had abandoned the idea."

"How did you get out?" I asked Michaela.

"There was an enormous padlock on it, so I put a hand grenade between the shackles and blew it up. It was hard to open, but I got it this far and was able to squeeze under it, where Max was waiting for me."

So that's why Max knew where to go.

"You opened it with a hand grenade?" asked Briggs incredulously.

"It's the only thing that worked."

Briggs just shook his head.

"What does it look like in there?" asked Joe.

"This is a tunnel that goes back a long way—as far back as we just came. It opens up at the end into a large room. That's where the boxes are. From there is a door that leads to a room with all kinds of weapons—pistols, rifles, machine guns, and hand grenades. In that room is the door the man, Hagen, went through."

"So, there's no door at the end of the tunnel?" I asked. "It just becomes wider?"

"Yes," said Michaela.

She was probably thinking, *I just said that. Doesn't Scott ever pay attention?*

"Okay, I was just making sure."

I figured I better cover myself just in case she really was thinking that.

"Let's pull it open," said Joe. "We go as fast and as silently as we can. Remember, any sound will be amplified in the tunnel. When we get to the end, we can evaluate the situation."

"Then let's go," said Briggs.

Together, we pulled the door up another couple of feet. We would have opened it completely, except it creaked as it moved. We were sure it couldn't be heard at the end, but there was no sense in tempting fate.

We rolled under it and started down the tunnel at a run.

I would have told Michaela to stay behind, but to what end? If it was going to blow up, the blast would probably travel down the tunnel—especially if they all blew. Also, Michaela was responsible for finding this entrance, so she deserved to be in on the finish.

Besides, she wouldn't have listened anyway.

Chapter 47

Hagen gave a little smile as he closed the door on his employer. What satisfaction!

And yet, it was bittersweet. How satisfying was it, really? The cancer diagnosis had hit him hard. Some people in that situation could look back at their lives with pride. Maybe they raised children or had a job they loved. Perhaps they had made a difference in the world, even in a small way. Or maybe they could look back and know they had lived an honest life.

Hagen had none of that. He got sucked into Prescott's life. He was well-paid for his efforts, but all that meant was that the more money Prescott paid him, the more trapped he was, making it harder and harder to leave. He was nothing more than a prisoner. He had never married—or even come close. He certainly hadn't lived a fulfilled life. Hell, he worked for an arms dealer, for Christ's sake! Yes, Prescott paid him well, but who reaped the benefits of Hagen's hard work? Prescott, of course.

It was appropriate that Prescott was known as "The Ghost." In a short time, he would be one for real.

Luckily for Hagen, he was one of the people holding a lantern when they all traveled down the tunnel under the shack. So, when he escaped through the door, he wasn't plunged into blackness.

Looking around him, he was amazed by the number of weapons piled high in the open crates. Impressive to some degree, but nowhere near the quality of weapons he had encountered over the years. This was yard sale junk. And some group thought they would be able to take over the United States with this crap? It was almost laughable. No, it *was* laughable.

But where were the Davey Crocketts? There had to be another room. Wouldn't it be funny if, after all this, it turned out that there weren't any?

He saw another door and headed toward it. As he got closer to the door, it seemed a bit darker. Why would that be?

Hagen looked down at his lantern. It wasn't as bright as before. Shit! The batteries were running down. He had to hurry. He pulled open the door and went through it carefully. After all, he didn't know what to expect. What if an animal was waiting for him on the other side?

No. No animals.

He was in another room—a much larger room connected to a tunnel on the other side. Of course! That's how they got the weapons in here. They landed in the valley nearest the shack, transported the weapons to the tunnel, and brought them in that way.

He looked around. The room was full of closed wooden crates. Some of the crates were labeled *M-28 Davy Crockett*, and others were labeled *M388/W54*. That was the M388 projectile with the W54 nuclear warhead. That's what he was looking for.

The boxes were sealed tight. He needed a crowbar, and he had to find it quickly. His light was noticeably weaker. There, against the wall, was a crowbar. He grabbed it, returned to the box of M388s, and pried off the lid.

There it was—the M388. He had never seen one before, but he was used to dealing with much more sophisticated weapons. It was a little less than a yard long and a foot wide at its widest. It had fins in the rear.

Hagen tried to remember what he knew about the M388. It wasn't much. He thought there was some kind of time delay switch in the back under the fins. But it also had some safety features, probably so someone like him didn't accidentally set it off.

He had a multi-purpose tool in a holster attached to his belt. He took it out and opened it to a screwdriver. If he could get the cover off, he could figure out how to detonate it.

It was suddenly much darker than a minute earlier. The batteries were fading fast. Where were the screws?

Suddenly, the light was down to a faint glow. Hagen cried with frustration and threw the tool down. It was impossible. He'd never get it to detonate.

He put his face in his hands and began to cry. They were tears of anger and frustration. But something else, too.

He suddenly realized that they were also tears of relief. He didn't want to kill all those other people. Prescott was his only target. The others didn't have to die as well.

His life had been one of futility. And now he was going to die a slow, painful death from the cancer. No, he didn't have to do that. Even in the pitch black, he could find his way to the other room. He remembered where the handguns were and had seen some ammo next to them. He didn't have to fill a whole clip. He just needed one bullet. That would be enough.

Just one.

Chapter 48

As we approached the end of the tunnel and the area with the Davy Crocketts, we turned out our lights and proceeded slowly. We didn't want to alert Hagen to our presence.

We walked slowly and carefully. Other than the train tracks, though, it was pretty smooth. But it was pitch black—so much so that my eyes couldn't even adjust to the darkness.

We reached the end of the tunnel. Something was wrong. There was no light. If Hagen were there, he'd have to have a light to detonate a bomb.

Then we heard the crack of a gun. I instinctively ducked. I'm sure the others did, too, but I couldn't see them. The gunshot sounded close.

"That came from the other room," said Michaela, "the one with the weapons. There's a door that leads to it."

"Lights on," said Briggs. "He's not in here."

We turned the lanterns back on. I felt some relief in doing so. I never realized before that moment that I was a bit claustrophobic. We walked tentatively into the area with the crates. The memo that Natalya had wasn't kidding—a large number had been stolen. No wonder they were worried back then.

"Looks like he was about to work on one," said Joe, "but he

never even got the cover off the projectile. He left a tool here, as well as his lamp."

We all moved over to the door. I had a sneaking suspicion about what we'd find. After all, the man said he had cancer.

I was right. I opened the door and threw my light in while Briggs and Joe entered the room the way I always saw cops do it in the movies. They looked good doing it. I think it was second nature for them both.

Hagen was lying on the floor, and there was blood everywhere. He had stuck the gun in his mouth and pulled the trigger. While there was sadness about it, there was also a sense of relief. The bombs were safe.

I guess none of us were paying attention to Prescott. He suddenly grabbed Hagen's gun with one hand and wrapped his other arm around Michaela's neck, pulling her to the door leading into the area under the building with the rooms. The gun barrel was against Michaela's head.

"Who's the pilot?" he demanded.

"I am," I said.

"You're going to open this door, then walk through it. Then I'm coming through with the girl. Bring a lantern. When we're through, you close the door, then walk ahead of us. If anyone comes through the door behind us, I'll kill the girl."

"But then you'll be killed," I said.

"At that point, it won't matter," he said. "But I know you care about the girl, so you'll do as I say."

I had no choice. Michaela was the only priority.

"I'm sure my pilot left when he heard the gunfire. He's a coward. So, when we get outside, we're going to your plane or one of the other planes out there, and you'll fly me out of here. Then I'll let you and the girl go."

I knew that wouldn't happen, but I had to bide my time. I

did as he said. As I closed the door, Joe nodded to me to say they'd think of something and be there for me. I had no doubt that they would try everything. But with Michaela's life on the line, I couldn't think about anything else.

He had me walk in front of him. He kept a tight grip on Michaela. Her eyes were wide with fear. I felt for her, but there was nothing I could do. And I knew how she felt. Having a gun pointed at your head is terrifying. I think at that point, Prescott no longer cared about the weapons—he knew he'd never get them. He just wanted to get out of there.

I reached the ladder at the trapdoor.

"You go first," said Prescott. "When you reach the top, you tell everyone to back away. And let my men go."

I started to climb the ladder. I realized I still had my gun and Michaela still had hers, but I couldn't take advantage of that.

Behind me, I heard Prescott say, "And you, little girl, better not try anything as we go up the steps. I *will* kill you."

I reached the top and saw Jon and Jess.

"Back away," I said. "Prescott is coming up with Michaela. He says he'll kill her if we try anything."

I didn't say anything about Prescott's men. If they went free, they'd probably kill Ollie's men, and I couldn't let that happen.

Prescott made it to the top awkwardly. He almost lost his grip on Michaela, but not enough for anyone to do anything. He was breathing heavily. I'd almost forgotten that he was in his seventies. This had to be strenuous for him. I think Michaela knew it, too. His grip had loosened a little—but not enough for her to make a move. And I really hoped she wouldn't make one.

Prescott looked out the door and saw his men kneeling on

the ground with their hands on their heads.

"I said to let them go," he said to me.

"No," I replied. "You have Michaela as your insurance, and we have your men as ours."

Prescott hesitated for a minute, then nodded his agreement. I'm sure that made the two men he had left pretty pissed.

"Okay, but no false moves," said Prescott.

It wasn't a false move that ended it, but rather, a hole. As they went out the door, Michaela stepped into a hole and lost her footing. She let out a cry. As she fell, she started to bring Prescott down with her. In a moment of panic, or maybe it was just a natural reaction for him, he pulled the trigger. The gun clicked. No explosion. No bullet in Michaela's brain.

Just as he pulled the trigger, Max came flying through the air like the comic book character Superdog and chomped on Prescott's wrist. Prescott let out a scream, but as he did so, he grabbed Michaela's .9mm from her holster and turned to shoot me, with Max still hanging on his arm. As Prescott turned, his head exploded, spraying blood all over me.

It seems that Briggs—who had just arrived on the scene after running back through the tunnel—and Jon shot at the same time, with both bullets penetrating Prescott's head. At the same time, the two prisoners jumped up and tried to disarm Ollie's men. Both received bullets for their efforts. They were dead before they hit the ground.

At that moment, Joe and Ollie showed up with guns drawn. They seemed disappointed to have missed the finale.

I went over to Michaela and hugged her. She was crying, but I think it was more from her ankle than from the experience of almost dying. I took a quick look at it. It was at least a bad sprain, but an X-ray would tell us if there was a broken bone.

I looked at Max. Like me, he was covered in blood. But also, like me, it was Prescott's blood. Max wasn't happy about being so dirty.

Jon picked up Prescott's pistol.

"Not loaded," he said. "There's not even a clip in it. Hagen had only put one round in the gun."

"That makes sense," I said. "It was a gun Hagen got from the weapons room. His intention—which he followed through on—was to commit suicide. He only needed one round for that. Prescott didn't even notice the missing magazine."

I looked around me.

Was it finally over?

Prescott was dead, as was his right-hand man. We figured out that Hagen killed himself because his light died. At that point, there was no way he could set off a bomb. And with an agonizing road ahead of him with his cancer, it was probably a lot easier this way. Just out of curiosity, Joe had taken the battery cover off when we were in the tunnel. They were the original batteries installed by the lantern manufacturer. No one had changed them out. Thank God for crappy batteries.

Let's see, who else was dead? We found the bodies of the woman and her three henchmen. Michaela said the KGB contractors who kidnapped her were responsible for that.

The great Mexican stand-off resulted in the deaths of the various contractors from the KGB, CIA, and Mossad, as well as a couple of Prescott's men—the rest of whom died with Prescott. I counted twenty dead, but I might have missed one or two. Holy cow! I could probably expect a visit from Child Services at some point. What? Didn't every parent bring their child into a war zone? I couldn't be the only one.

Jon and Jess came over and gave me hugs.

"We were able to get close-up views of all the skeletons,"

said Jess. "Luckily, the door must've always been closed, and there were no windows in the building, so large animals couldn't get in and destroy the bones. One of the skeletons must have belonged to a munitions worker. He had no identification, and his tattered clothes looked like something a worker would wear. Two of them might have been wearing military fatigues. Prescott was right about one of the skeletons—as far as we could tell, it was his father, The Russian. And the last one solves one of the most talked about of all mysteries. It was Chat Olson, the band's manager."

"You're kidding," I said.

"We think there was a shoot-out between Olson and The Russian," said Jon. "I guess how and why they both ended up here will never be known. We found something interesting though. In one of Olson's pockets was a key—it looks like a safe deposit box key. With a little cleaning up, we might be able to get some information about it."

"Not that it will do any good," said Briggs. "Unless he paid sixty years in advance, that box was opened years ago, with the contents sent to their unclaimed office. When no one claimed it, the contents were probably destroyed."

"Probably?" I asked.

Briggs sighed. "Okay, I'll look into it. But later. I wasn't here."

I wondered what the real story about Olson was. Were Olson and The Russian partners who had a falling out? Everything I'd ever read about Olson in my recent research led me to say no. He sounded like a standup guy. So, what was the story?

And would we ever know?

Chapter 49

We had some decisions to make. Like Briggs said, he wasn't here. He was on vacation. I checked quickly and found that both rounds exited Prescott's head and landed somewhere in the woods. So his gun couldn't be tied to this.

We decided that I would call Briggs's official phone when we got home to report what happened. Briggs could then grab some of his men and investigate the incident. I would give him the safe deposit box key at that point.

Ollie and his guys would head home as soon as we arrived in Homer. Like Briggs, they were also never there. As much as Joe preferred to stay in the background, he decided to stay. We had to explain how we were able to kill so many people. Although, the KGB, CIA, and Mossad contractors, with Prescott's help, had wiped each other out—we didn't have a hand in that. Jon, Jess, Michaela, and I—and of course, Max the Wonder Dog—would do most of the explaining.

I realized that I would have to fly back with Michaela and Max and then come back for the others. My plane was bigger than my previous one, but it was not big enough for that group.

But first, I had to wash the blood from Max and me.

Jess decided to accompany us and take Michaela to the hospital to have her ankle examined. Briggs came, too, to get back in time to establish his alibi.

I returned to Homer, dropped off Jess and Michaela at the hospital, and was preparing my plane for the return trip when my SAT phone rang. It was Jon.

"Hey, bro, is there any way you can snag the helicopter for another trip?"

"Yeah, I think so."

I wondered where this was going.

"Can you land at the crash site instead of the valley?"

"Uh, sure. Why? To pick up the tents you left there?"

"No. We'll tell you when you get here."

"Okay. Anything you say."

I was confused at first, and then it hit me. I knew why he wanted me to do that.

Briggs did, too.

The cash.

"I'm a government agent. I don't want any of it," he said.

When I landed, Jon, Joe, Ollie, and his gang were there to meet me.

It was Ollie who brought it up.

"We were thinking. Remember how you said that Prescott told you his father sent someone on the band's plane with a briefcase filled with a million dollars?"

"I remember."

"And Briggs said it wasn't found in the wreckage, as far as he knew."

"Right," I said.

"Which means it should still be out here," said Ollie.

"It's certainly possible. Unless, of course, it broke open, and the money blew away. After sixty years, it would be long gone."

"Chances are," said Joe, "the suitcase wouldn't have been

cheap. It might still be here."

"And we'd just like to look around a bit," added Ollie.

"Is it legal?" I asked Joe.

"It's kind of a gray area," he replied. "Up until now, no one even knew about the arms deal. The million dollars wasn't stolen, although I'm sure none was obtained legally. So really, for all intents and purposes, it never existed."

"Well, I don't want any of it," I said. "Briggs figured out what you wanted to do and said he wants none of it."

"Jess and I don't want any of it, either," said Jon. "We have plenty of money."

"And I have no need for it," added Joe.

"Ollie, I guess that leaves you and your gang," I said.

"We're not proud," said Ollie with a smile. "We'll be happy to take it."

So we started our search. Like a poor man's NTSB, we recreated the crash. We figured out a triangular area in front of where the plane's nose ended up, figuring that since the suitcase wasn't in the plane, it would have flown forward from the crash and out the cockpit window. It was hard to figure out how far it would have sailed, but all we could do was look.

It took four hours, but to my amazement, we found it. One of Ollie's guys discovered it half buried in the dirt and under a tree. The large case might have ended up completely buried, except it landed where a tree was growing. The roots kept it above ground.

The suitcase was in pretty bad shape, but it was intact. I knocked off the rusted latch with a rock. I opened the case and gawked at dozens of wrapped packets of hundred-dollar bills.

I closed the case and pushed it over to Ollie.

"That should be enough payment for your work today," I said.

"What, no tip?" he replied with a big smile.

*****

As soon as we arrived home, Ollie—clutching the suitcase—and his boys hopped on their plane and took off. The sooner they were out of there, the better. It was a good haul for a day's work.

Briggs had taken a commercial puddle-jumper to Anchorage earlier to be ready for my phone call alerting him to the happenings at the cabin.

When I got home, Michaela was sitting in a chair with her leg propped up. She had a cast on her ankle.

"Well, aren't you special," I said, giving her a hug.

She had no biting retort to that.

"Broken?" I asked, pointing to the ankle.

"It is," answered Jess. "Not a bad one, though."

"You might want to call your friend, Sally, to let her know you're okay, but without revealing anything that went on," I said.

"I already did," Michaela answered.

"But she didn't go into any details," said Jess. "She told her that she'd explain it later."

"Good."

I got a call from Briggs on his burner phone. He had landed in Anchorage and was all settled back in his apartment.

"Okay," I said. "Let's get this show on the road."

I called Briggs on his official phone.

"Special Agent Briggs, this is Scott Harper."

"Hi, Scott. How can I help you?"

"I have to report something to you…"

Chapter 50

I called a press conference.

Me. The guy who just wants to be left alone actually called a press conference. Yeah, that guy.

I had no choice. I had to make sure these things were disposed of correctly. If those nukes went off, some of the most beautiful landscape in the world would become a crater. I didn't know what would happen to the weapons once the military learned about them. Not that I'm not a trusting guy, but, well… I'm not. I had just experienced too much greed. I couldn't trust anyone. And since I was the one who found it, I felt it was my responsibility.

Transparency is a popular word these days. Well, here was an example where transparency was vital. If the press and the world knew about these weapons, they could be dismantled and destroyed safely. No secrets and no conspiracies.

Joe's boss, celebrity lawyer Mill Colson, helped me set up the press conference. When Mill talked, people listened. And unlike some backwoods bush pilot like me, Mill could make sure the FBI, CIA, and others wouldn't interfere in my holding the press conference.

Speaking of the FBI, as far as they were concerned, Briggs had been on vacation and knew nothing of this. His boss had suspicions but couldn't do anything about it. Briggs's involvement would forever remain anonymous.

In addition, the CIA had no clue of Marty Young's involvement. The back channel between Marty and Briggs remained secure.

The press conference went well. I held it in Anchorage so reporters wouldn't inundate Homer. This was an exciting time for the media. The discovery of *The Wonder Boys* followed quickly by the discovery of stolen nuclear weapons almost sixty years earlier that the public had no knowledge of. And I was about to blow them away with the news that the events were all connected.

As much as I hated the press and wanted to remain in the background, I wasn't nervous when I stepped up in front of the microphone. Too much had happened, and frankly, I was sick of the secrecy. Some of the press remembered my name from the Wisdom Spring incident, but I didn't want to bring up any of that.

"My name is Scott Harper. As most of you know by now, I was the pilot who, along with my daughter and my dog"—hey, I had to give Max some of the credit—"discovered the wreckage of the plane carrying the band, *The Wonder Boys*. Two miles from that site, we discovered a bunker containing nuclear weapons dating back to the same period. Most of you are aware by now of both discoveries. What you may not know is that the two events are related. More will come out about it in time, but what you need to know is that the deaths of *The Wonder Boys* was calculated. Basically, they were in the wrong place at the wrong time. *The Wonder Boys* died needless deaths because of greed—the greed of nations obsessed about nuclear weapons."

I had their attention.

"In the secret bunker—although, not so secret anymore—are enough nuclear weapons to do serious damage. Many people have died in the quest for those weapons. I was witness to many of the deaths. These people were private contractors hired by various governments—including our own—and by arms dealers. By hiring contractors, the countries could claim that they knew nothing about it.

"An international watchdog agency is overseeing the dismantling and disposal of the weapons, but my purpose in having this news conference is to make everyone aware of what is going on, so that there can be no cover-ups."

I laid out the whole experience and told them everyone involved—independent contractors from the CIA, KGB, and Mossad, arms dealer Prescott (AKA The Ghost), his father, The Russian, and others. And then to find out that the events were related to the deaths of *The Wonder Boys* took the news to another level altogether. Adding to that the discovery of Chat Olson, and it became a feeding frenzy.

Okay, I didn't lay out the whole experience. I mentioned a KGB agent finding the facility in 2010, but I didn't give her name, and I certainly didn't say that she was Michaela's mother.

Like it or not, Michaela's name couldn't be left out. However, I let the press know in no uncertain terms that should any of them attempt to interview her, there were a lot of people and one very protective dog who would not allow that to happen. In fact, Ollie and his men offered to come down to Homer to act as bodyguards for her. I thanked them but let them know it wasn't necessary. The Piney Lake crowd were also not mentioned in the press conference.

It was kind of funny how many people helped us out but didn't want to be connected in any way. So, all I could say about them at the press conference was to acknowledge the help of "many others," all of whom wished to remain anonymous. That created a lot of rumors and speculation in the press, which we all found funny.

As much as I hated my exposure to the press—and the world—the press conference did its job. The bombs were being dismantled as I spoke. The U.S. government said they would have destroyed the weapons anyway, and I believed them. I'm sure they would have.

But I had to do it this way.

Chapter 51

A week had passed since the events at the bunker. Briggs was standing outside a bank in downtown Seattle.

Let's hope they don't laugh me out of here, he thought.

He entered the Willow Bank and flashed his badge to the security guard.

"I need to speak to the bank manager," he said.

"Sure. Right in that office," said the guard, pointing to an open door.

"Thanks."

Briggs sucked in some air and muttered, "Here goes nothing."

He knocked on the open door, flashed his badge, and said, "Special Agent Duane Briggs of the FBI. Do you have a moment?"

"Uh, sure."

Briggs almost laughed. The guy looked like he was about to wet his pants. He couldn't have been more than a year or two out of college, and looked even younger than that. He was wearing an ill-fitting suit and had a short haircut.

"Don't worry. You're not in any trouble. I'm just looking for a little information."

"Sure. What can I help you with?"

The voice had a squeak to it.

"We've recovered a safe deposit box key for this bank. The problem is, it's almost sixty years old."

The manager's eyes opened wide.

"Sixty years?"

"Yeah. I realize it's a shot in the dark, but I'm hoping you might still have possession of the contents of the unclaimed box."

"You're joking, right?"

"I wish I were."

"I have no idea how to find that out."

Great! I'm going to have to walk this guy every step of the way.

"Well, how about you call someone who might know."

"Uh. I'm not sure…"

"It's important," said Briggs, suddenly putting on his FBI intimidation face. "Call your unclaimed property division."

It took almost an excruciating hour, but finally the manager—with a lot of prompting from Briggs—reached the right person. He directed Briggs to a place in the warehouse district.

When Briggs arrived, he was met by an older man with round glasses. Briggs thought he looked like a librarian, which seemed appropriate. He explained the situation.

"Sixty years, huh?"

"Almost. It was 1966. Is there any way it could still be around?"

"Doubtful. If it's too old, most of this stuff eventually gets destroyed. But I've been surprised before. Let's see the key."

It had been cleaned up by people in the FBI lab.

"Number 447," said the man, writing it down. "And the name attached to it?"

"Probably Chatwell Olson."

"Chatwel... *The Wonder Boys*?"

"The same. It's really important that we find it, if it's still around."

"I get it. I loved *The Wonder Boys*. I'll do what I can. Give me a few hours. This is what I have to work with."

He opened a door to a back room. It was piled high with boxes.

"Yikes," said Briggs.

Briggs gave him his card.

"It's a needle in a haystack, but I'm hoping it still exists," he said.

"I'll call you as soon as I know."

Three hours later, his phone rang.

"Found it."

*****

I was washing down my plane when my phone rang.

"I thought you should be the first to know," began Briggs. "You should hear the information before we release it to the press."

"Something good?" I asked.

"You might say that. As much as I hate to admit it, your suggestion of tracking down the safe deposit key paid off."

"Hate to admit it because I was right and you were wrong?"

He ignored me.

"It was a Seattle-based bank. They were still in the same location downtown. Almost unheard of these days. The unclaimed items from safe deposit boxes were stored away and forgotten. However, I found someone there who thought he would play detective. Even he admitted that the chances of finding anything were slim. But in the end, he came through. He showed me the room everything is stored in. It reminded me of a smaller version of the final warehouse scene in Raiders of the Lost Ark. Stuff was everywhere. But somehow he was able to track it down.

"There was only one thing in the box—a handwritten letter sealed in an envelope. I don't know whether Olson expected to come back and do something with it, or if he knew he wasn't coming back and assumed that when the box went unclaimed, someone would find it. Who knows? But in the letter, he laid out everything he knew."

"Which was?"

"Prescott's father—the arms dealer known as The Russian—was behind it, as we already knew. He gave us the names of two people who were murdered and whose deaths are probably cold cases—a Nancy Baldwin and Alvin Dickson. Baldwin was Olson's girlfriend. She was murdered by someone in The Russian's organization. Dickson was an associate of The Russian and was killed by Olson in retaliation for his girlfriend's death. I looked them up and he was right—neither death was ever solved. He mentions hiring Travis Miller as a roadie for the band, but then suspecting that he was involved with The Russian. He also wrote that minutes before the ill-fated flight to Fairbanks, he allowed a CIA agent to board the plane. That would have been Linus Cutter."

"Does it say how he ended up dead in Alaska?" I asked.

"Yeah, he wrote this after he died."

Before I could swear at him, he laughed and said, "I know what you mean. He said he found out the location and was going to charter a plane to take him there. He said he would probably never find The Russian, but he could exact some revenge on the people involved. Maybe he didn't expect The Russian to be there."

"So, Chat Olson was a hero," I said.

"Looks like it. We also raided Prescott's home on Long Island and found meticulous records. A lot of people are going down because of those records."

"Three-letter agencies, too?"

"Yeah, well…"

I got it.

Some things would never be revealed.

Epilogue

I went home and told Michaela about the letter. She had been quiet since returning home from the bunker, but I thought it was important to give her the space she needed. But after telling her about the letter, Michaela asked if we could take a walk.

That wasn't an activity we usually engaged in, so I knew it meant that she wanted to talk about something. And I had a feeling I knew what it was. Michaela was finally going to let it out. She insisted on walking, even with a walking boot and a crutch. I figured it must be serious.

We took the trail to the cliffs without a word spoken between us. Slob stayed in front of us, searching the woods for any dangerous animals, and a freshly washed Max stayed at Michaela's side. He had picked up on her mood and wanted her to know that he was there for her.

We sat at the edge of a cliff and looked out at Kachemak Bay. Michaela took my hand. At thirteen, she could either be an adult or a child. The child was coming out.

"Did my mom love me?"

Yup, I knew that was coming.

"Of course she loved you. I never met her, but even I know how important you were to her. You were her life."

"But she was a spy."

"I think they refer to them as operatives, but yes, she was one."

"She never told me."

"She didn't want you to know about that world. It's an ugly world, and she only wanted beauty for you.

"Was my mother a bad person?"

I chuckled. "Do you think Joe is a bad person?"

"Of course not."

"He was a spy—or operative—just like your mother."

"But he was with the CIA. My mother was with the KGB."

"And?"

"The KGB is bad."

"And the CIA is good? Michaela, you were right in the middle of it. You saw these groups—these agencies—fighting over weapons meant to destroy people. They may have all been independent contractors, but they were hired by the agencies to cover their tracks. What does that tell you about them? I'm sure they all had their excuses why it should be them and not the others who should take possession of the weapons. But in the end, it was all about power and greed. They were all the same."

She nodded but kept her eyes looking at the ground. I hadn't convinced her yet.

"Your mother was young when she joined the KGB. She was idealistic and was probably sold on the excitement of the life. By the time she got pregnant with you, she had grown and matured. Suddenly, she realized that there was something more important. And that something was you."

Not convinced yet.

"Your mother would have done anything for you. She would have killed for you. In fact, I think you picked up some of your mother's traits and skills. You killed for her. When we were stuck out in the wilderness a few months ago, you told me about the man who came into your house when your mother was sick with cancer. He was looking for the old Russian seaman's logbook. There was no hesitation on your part. In fact, you emptied a whole magazine into him, if I remember right."

"One bullet missed."

She was beginning to perk up.

"Yeah, well, you'll have to work on that. That'll be your next assignment."

"Delegating again?"

"It's what I do."

Michaela put her head on my shoulder, and Max put his head on Michaela's shoulder.

"My mother, the spy," said Michaela.

"It has a nice ring to it, doesn't it?"

"It kinda does."

Max gave out a loud sigh.

"But I think I'm where I belong now," said Michaela.

"You are."

The End

AUTHOR'S NOTE:

The M28 (and M29) Davy Crockett Weapon System was a real weapon. It used an M388 projectile armed with a W54 nuclear warhead. Put into service in 1961, it was one of the smallest nuclear weapons ever built. With a firing range of 1.25 miles (M28) and 2.5 miles (M29) and a blast yield of up to 20 tons of TNT, it was designed to be used on the front lines by the infantry. The M28/M29 Davy Crockett Weapon System was never used in combat and was retired in 1971.

About the Author

Andrew Cunningham is the author of 19 novels, including the *"Lies" Mystery Series*: **All Lies, Fatal Lies, Vegas Lies, Secrets & Lies, Blood Lies, Buried Lies,** and **Sea of Lies;** the post-apocalyptic *Eden Rising Series*: **Eden Rising, Eden Lost, Eden's Legacy,** and **Eden's Survival;** the *Yestertime Time Travel Series:* **Yestertime, The Yestertime Effect, The Yestertime Warning,** and **The Yestertime Shift;** the disaster/terrorist thriller **Deadly Shore,** and the *Alaska Thrillers Series*: **Wisdom Spring, Nowhere Alone,** and **The 7th Passenger.** As A.R. Cunningham, he has written a series of five children's mysteries in the *Arthur MacArthur* series. Born in England, Andrew was a long-time resident of Cape Cod. He and his wife now live in Florida. Please visit his website at **Arcnovels.com**, his Facebook page, **Author Andrew Cunningham**, and his **Amazon Author Page**.

Printed in Great Britain
by Amazon